WILL WEST

by Paul C. Metcalf

THE BOOKSTORE PRESS
Lenox, Mass.

Copyright 1956 by Paul C. Metcalf.
First Edition published by Jonathan Williams,
Asheville, North Carolina, 1956

Second Edition © Copyright 1973 by Paul C. Metcalf
Cover Illustration by Bob Totten
Printed by Studley Press, Inc.

ISBN No. 0-912846-03-8

Other books by Paul Metcalf:

GENOA and PATAGONI
both published by Jonathan Williams

APALACHE
to be published, Spring 1974, by Swallow Press

for Nancy

ONE

Will stood on the mound, waiting, his feet planted apart. The two numerals sewn in thick maroon to the back of his shirt, felt heavy. Number 19. Across his chest, in shorter maroon, armpit to collarbone to armpit, were six letters: R E B E L S. His gray flannel uniform was trimmed in maroon, and heavy maroon socks rose above his ankles, almost to the droop of his pants on his shins. He was hot, sweating under the four banks of lights, under the flannel uniform, the cotton underwear, sweating hard. His feet were tight in the black, spiked shoes. But his arm felt loose and rubbery.

"G'wan! G'wan! Pitch to him!"

The crowd was landing on him. Two or three thousand, perhaps. There were some Indian calls. But he waited. Under the visor of his cap, his quiet eyes looked down the trail, the path of red smooth dirt that led from the mound through the infield grass to home plate. He waited, without motion, and watched for the sign.

The catcher was waiting, too. Standing, not crouching. Will was in trouble. The eighth inning, a run already in and the lead gone,

Men on the bases. The crowd, the home crowd, whooping it up. The catcher stood in front of the plate, looking around, hollering orders to the infield, his mask held in his hand. He was fat, and the chest protector made him look fatter. He gestured with the mask to the first baseman and then the third baseman, and they punched their gloves and danced a few steps in response to orders they couldn't possibly hear. It was a good ritual, holding up the game, and the crowd loved it. A fat catcher, when there's no more baseball left in him, can still get by as an actor.

This was the bush. The game was rough and simple, not machine-like, as in the majors. These boys had played baseball since they could walk. Played it until their legs gave out, or they couldn't fight off the extra flesh any more; until their arms turned from rubber to glass. . .

Will was motionless, waiting. The catcher glowered around the infield, then turned toward the mound, and stepped forward. But Will didn't come down to meet him, so he stopped and turned toward the plate. The man in blue, short and stocky, was waiting, jaw thrust forward, hands clasped behind his back. The catcher went back to his position, and the crowd yelled, raucous. He turned to face Will, and put on his mask. Slowly, he let down his weight, went into a crouch, and lifted the bottom flap of the body protector. In front of the gray flannel stretched tight around his bottom, he lowered three fingers, and gave the sign.

Will moved, lifted one leg, drew his feet together. The banks of lights over the first and third base stands flooded directly upon him, and he was aware of the others, over the bleachers, pouring on his back. Shifting his weight to one foot, he began smoothing and re-arranging the loose earth of the mound with the toe cleats of the other. A slow, softshoe dance, with his glove hand on his hip, and his pitching hand holding the ball loosely at his side; his head declined, his figure arrogantly modest and indifferent. A pebble here, a pile of dirt there: building, smoothing, leveling the surface. The earth mound, he thought, surrounded by a forest of grass, the trails through the forest, and beyond, the howling wilds . . . turning, swirling, curving, the toe of the shoe. . . .

They're starting the Indian calls again not because they have anything against me but because that's the easiest handle to put on me because that's what I am an Indian a Cherokee Indian. Smoky they call me in the papers partly in derision because my fast ball isn't very fast and partly because that's where I come from the Qualla Boundary the Cherokee Reservation in the Great Smoky Mountains of Western North Carolina. The Great Smokies where the summers are cool not hot like here in the low country not the tropical miasmic cloud of heat that hangs low over the land six months of the year that even the ocean can't dispel that spreads to the first row of dunes on the beach the heat that I live in all summer to pitch for this low country town. In the dugout to the left sit the home players in their white uniforms lined on the bench like dummies or like puppets with their arms and legs moved by strings from above. Their faces hidden from the lights against the concrete backwall are as ruddy as mine and motionless watching me waiting for me. The grandstands are full and even the white-coated coke sellers turn to look. On the right beyond the grandstand are the negro faces drawn together and isolated from the others. So I've got to pitch. Men on bases. The lead gone. And the sign. . . .

Will stopped sweeping the dirt with his foot and looked up. His eyes went down the trail and the catcher gave the sign again. Three fingers. A slow outside curve that drops in, cuts the outside corner. The crowd was howling now, many of them on their feet. Behind him, the shortstop and second baseman chanted encouragement. The fingers of his pitching hand flexed around the ball . . . but something in him would not begin. Again, his head went down, and the toe cut little paths in the surface of the mound . . .

Because I'm an Indian and sometimes they question me when I get into a bus question which race I'm to sit with. Smoky Will. Smoky Will West Cherokee Indian pitcher. Full-blooded but not quite there was that fake Irishman that Scotchman who went to live in Ireland for a while and got himself called Scotch-Irish the one who came across the Atlantic water in a sailing ship landed at Baltimore or maybe up the river at Philadelphia but whichever it was cut out across Pennsylvania which was still wild country got to the Alleghanies the Appalachian range and liked the natural flow of

3

those north-south valleys he was a hill man a Scotch highlander with tight lips a thin face an eagle's nose and watery blue eyes he knew the north mountains the rough unyielding rocks but his blood needed warming so he turned south. Got himself a coonskin cap and put a feather in it a buckskin jacket and pants with leather trimming just like an Indian a rifle and powder horn and a horse to carry his belongings carry the trinkets and likker he bought to trade to the Indians for skins yes that was before the Removal and there were still Indians in the mountains they'd been pushed back but they were strong in the mountains just the Indians and the traders and the poachers. Maybe he drank at that spring on the edge of Indian country that the traders all consider unlucky they said if you drink at that spring on your way in you won't come out for weeks you'll go on a rootintootin bender get yourself an Indian girl or maybe two or three get drunk and then get drunker and just stay right on drunk. Maybe he drank at that spring. I don't know. But in any case he got in and he stayed in. Smoky Will West has that Scotchman in his blood.

The yelling had a different tone: angry, derisive. He had overplayed the delay. When he looked up, the man in blue had stepped in front of the plate and was approaching, walking up the trail toward the mound. He was short, with heavy shoulders, a large head, and large blue eyes. He stopped halfway, and gestured.

"Play ball!" he yelled.

He turned and walked back in short steps, head and shoulders erect, to his position.

Will had watched him, had made no acknowledgement. He watched him retreat down the path. Then he took his position on the rubber. His muscles moved slowly, they didn't want to try. He poised himself, his hands held before him with ball and glove against the letters across his chest. He could take no wind-up, there were men on base. He glanced at first. Both players were dancing nervously, but they were different: the baserunner sporting like a clown, putting on a show; the fielder really nervous, his feet lifting lightly, the motion springing from the pit of his stomach, almost uncontrollable. Will's eyes swept across his chest, over the white ball clutched in his dark glove, and out to third base. The runner in his white uniform, his face pallid in the full flood of lights, looked like a phantom against the negro bleachers. The fielder made a flurry toward the base, and the runner responded with a flurry. Just a form, Will thought. They're not really trying. He turned toward home. The batter waited, his bat held back off his shoulder. The catcher was raised part way out of his crouch; he thrust his mitt forward, as though pushing something away from him: challenging Will. Over his shoulder, like a sun resting on the shoulder of a mountain before lifting into the sky, was the large head of the man in blue.

The crowd yelled in unabated anger. Will thought of Chief Bender, the great Indian pitcher, of a trick he'd pull when things were going rough, when the crowd got on him. He'd step off the mound and amble toward the stands 'Listen,' he'd say; 'I'm running things here. If you don't like it, why don't you go back where you came from?' And he thought of Ol' Bobo's remark: My stuff was good, they were just hitting it.'

He lifted his arms over his head in the stretch, the ball held in the glove. His muscles felt loose and rubbery and good. The sweat drenching his body and his clothes helped him, he thought. They wouldn't get a loud foul off me, if I could bring myself to try. . . .

He lowered his arms into the final pose. Again the quick, almost surreptitious glance at first and third. In each case, the runner gave him a little flurry. His arm jerked back and the muscle felt free and powerful all the way. As his body wheeled in support of the arm, he could see the white-flanneled runner on third faking for home. A deep breath seemed to catch in his throat, to dry it suddenly, at the nadir of his backward motion. . . .

It is those of us who cannot untangle ourselves from the past that are really dangerous in the present because we are only partly here our eyes are blind because our appetites are turned inward or backward chewing on the cold remnants of our inheritance of our facts of our history to try to find who we are what we are where we came from what is the ground we stand on to whom does it belong and did it belong. We are dangerous because when we come out of the past we are rich with its energies and poorly experienced in the business of daily living and we hurl ourselves across the present with the blind fierceness of a martyr or a convert defending our damage to the defenseless with a language they cannot understand a language created from false concepts of time of history of past present and future. In the end we will bring to the world nothing useful and although we may find what we have been and even what we are nevertheless for all our search the heavy helpless stumbling of men born in quicksand we will never know what we have done.

As his arm swung forward in a half sidearm motion, the length and weight of his body following it, pivoting on his left leg, the breath charged from him, and his throat felt hot. He was aware all the way of the free grip of his hand on the surface of the ball, of the healthy feeling of the muscles in his arm. He felt capable, 'right.' His wrist flicked, as his hand reached the end of its forward penetration, and his fingers spread: the ball went spinning from them. His right foot struck the forward slope of the mound, and his weight came to rest heavily. His throwing hand, completing its arc, swung back and forth loosely, hanging as though the arm had broken. He waited.

In the moment the ball spun from the cup of his hand, Will knew two things. First that the pitch was good. It would do what it was supposed to: float outside, and then break, cut in at the last minute, catch the outside corner. The speed, the delivery, the aim were right. And second, that the batter wouldn't be fooled. Caught in the fever of the rally, he'd set himself, was going to swing at the first pitch, good or bad. It was a good pitch, but it was the wrong one to call. 'My stuff was good, they were just hitting it.'

He waited, the hand swinging slowly, and watched the batter swing, watched him reach outside to get it on the end of the bat. In the last instant, the ball cut in, as it had been told, and struck the bat on the fattest the healthiest part of the wood. The batter swung clean, pulled the pitch to left field. In the instant of the 'crack', the angry, individual yelling of the crowd, the dissonance of separate voices sank into an ocean of enthusiasm. Will watched the white pellet disappear like a shooting star over his right shoulder. He drew himself up, brought his feet together on the surface of the mound, and waited, hands on hips, head declined. He looked up only casually to watch the fielding of the ball, watch the white-flanneled figures fading around the third base corner, waved on by their coach. It was a solid smash, close to the foul line, good for a double or triple. The runner on third was in of course, and the man from first came all the way around and scored. The play, when it was finally made, was at the plate, and the batter came into third, radiant with motion and confidence, for a standing-up triple. Will looked down and began again the idle smoothing and re-arranging of loose earth on the surface of the mound.

The crowd was tumultuous. Individual voices were beginning to emerge out of the hum. Indian calls, riding on the crest of the noise, came to Will's ears. He didn't look up, but waited, the toe-cleat scraping over the dirt.

He didn't need to look up, he knew what was happening. The ball had not been returned to him, was held by the catcher. The catcher, perhaps a couple of infielders were approaching. From the dugout came an older man, a man with a uniform like his own, but with no number on the back: the Manager.

Something in him broke. Looking up abruptly, he stepped off the mound and headed toward the dugout. He didn't wait to be approached, to submit to the ritual of having the ball withheld from him, of being patted on the back to warm his confidence and keep it warm for his next effort, the next time he would pitch. Stepping off the mound, he voilated form, and wrote his own exit.

The manager had approached halfway, and stopped on the base path. Will glanced at him only briefly, at his surprised offended eyes, and walked past him without a word. Under a shower of derisive calls, he stepped into the dugout. He turned to the water fountain and drank deeply, let the water play over his face and into his mouth and throat. . . .

That is the last time I will stand on the mound will stand in the center under the four banks of lights. One day in the dead of winter when the ground is hard and the sky is gray and the parks are empty I will come down from the mountains to this or another field and I will walk out on the grass and up the path from home to the pitcher's mound and I will stand alone on the height of the earth and perhaps it will snow. I will face the black bare stands the boarded windows of the press box the empty dugouts the gray numberless lights darkly racked against the sky and I will let the snowflakes fall on my head and shoulders and off the backs of my empty hands. I will stand alone in the snow. . . .

TWO

Will went east,
   to where red dirt turns to pluff,
   and pluff to white, finegrain
   sand.

Sand and ocean.
Sand, sun and ocean,
   and unhorizoned clouds reaching high,

High, above the water — Will looked
   into a blind horizon.

Damn the gulls, with their embracing wings!
   damn
   the heron, curlew, kite and rail —
   merganser, grebe and gallinule!

God damn the tern and nigger goose!

The weather turns upon the weather
— midsummer handspring —
   and the ocean bakes a fish.
The sun is fat.

Turning to the land, Will discovered, across the sweep of beach, an approaching silhouette. The figure, despite distortions of lighting, was clearly that of a girl. She was walking up the beach away from town, planning to pass him, apparently, several yards in shore, toward the dunes. She followed a straight course, moving with athletic grace. He continued to watch her as she passed out of the distorted sunlight, came into her own substance and color. Her hair, dark brown, fell loosely across her shoulders. Her legs were long, slender at the calf, filling out within proportion at the groin and hips. She was tanned, but not too much, and wore a two-piece bathing suit, white. Her eyes, as he could make them out, were the color of her hair, and she had no make-up. Her breasts were firm.

Palmettos, rattling in a slow wind,
    draw back, back
    from winds of violence.

Sea oats fondle the air,
    and sand,
        singing a high song,
Stings the crust of sand.

        Will's foot
          is still,
        While water warms his toes,

        And on Will's back,
          the eastward back,
            sweat grows.

Dry sand fell from his feet and ankles as he ran across the hard beach, swinging in an arc to approach on the far side, the shore side. She kept her eyes forward and he saw only the flowing, richly curled hair on the back and sides of her head until he caught up with her and fell into her stride, his arm brushing against hers. Then she turned to him. She started to smile, but her face became suddenly serious and composed.

Now she knows she knows that I am an Indian not a stocky white youth burned in the sun but an Indian. This is the body these are the cheekbones the straight nose color not of the sun but of the man the body that played Indian ball game a mixture of football soccer lacrosse boxing wrestling played with sticks a hard ball no padding no shoes on a bare enormous stony field. . . .

The tide was low, and a wide hollow lay in their path, ridged by the action of earlier waves, holding at its centre a pool of captive ocean. At the far end, through a single outlet, the water flowed gradually outward. A jellyfish hovered near the outlet.

History is not made by fish,
   not by the bass,
   the mullet or the cat,

Not by the rugged-shelled oyster, or
   the jellyfish,
   holding off the tide,

Not by the stingaree!

At the water's edge, a broad sand bar curled into the ocean, standing just above the wave surface. The breakers parted in approaching, and lapped at its edges. Large gray gulls were gathered on it, and some took to flight, lifting themselves ponderously, drawing their legs to their bodies as they rose watchfully above sand and water. Those remaining on the sand crowded to the edge of the ocean, flapping their wings between flight and arrest, until Will and the girl had passed. Among the dunes, the palmettos became fewer and shorter, more wind-destroyed.

Will stopped suddenly, feet spread apart, and held the girl, his right arm gripping her waist, lifting her so that her toes barely touched the sand. With his left arm, he drew her shoulders toward him; she held him back, pressing both palms against his chest, and they became motionless, locked together.

From Will's crotch,
   apex of the sand-leg man,
   her legs descend,

A plumb line
to the white,
white sand.

Will's arm is stone,
and the man
— man and girl —
are
carved of sand,

Old figures cut against
salt,
high gull,
and wind.

Face to face, their eyes met, head on. Hers were dark and large and sober, framed in a tan face; they held Will's gaze steadily.

I to I,
thought of time,
and out of time,
of tide,
and beyond tide,

Red, and sun-fertile white
girl, girl, girl, girl,
the anger of nothing.

Although Will held her gaze, the edges of his vision neverthe less "pulled in" the surrounding landscape — the soft, dissolving curves, north and southward, of the beach.

And if the land be a map,
or the map a terrain,
And if a man be given,
or if a man uncover

What is the land, and
What is the form of the man?

If the map, of itself,
Be a form, a plan for

    the discovery of land,

What brings the land,
What brings the form of the man,

    into relief?

    As suddenly as he had stopped her, she broke and headed for the dunes. For a moment, he watched her, motionless. Then he started after her. The soft sand approaching the dunes slowed her: she leaned forward, propelling herself from the hips, swinging her arms awkwardly like a young gull struggling to learn flight. At the edge of the dunes he came up to her and caught her hand in his. They were panting and sweating as they trudged over the top and made their way among the dunes, up and down, around the patches of grass and briers. The wind descended to a whisper, and the air became sticky. Climbing to one of the higher points, they found a shady hollow directly behind it, and they jumped and skidded into the lowest part. Sitting down, facing oppositely, their hips touching, they swung their upper bodies in front of each other, and embraced hotly.

    There was no wind, and the sun was relentless.

Through grasses, snarling
    the earth, and

Briers,

Comes a murmer,
    captive:
    a murmer of wind.

Sweat,
    sweat and sea air

Separating, rising, they stood back from one another. Will's trunks, and the two pieces of the girl's white bathing suit, fell to the sand. For a moment they faced each other, naked in the hot sun and dampness, in the still air. With the exposure of the parts of her body hitherto covered, the girl gave a striped appearance — tan and white and tan and white and tan.

She made a gesture as though to run, a flurry, laughing a little, and he met it, halting her by implication. Again they hesitated, watching.

> The whirlpool at
>   the end of each breast
> Draws her life
>   into heavy, unwhirling air,
> and to the hardness of the man.

As they came together he held her around the waist, and she leaned back, pressing against him. Then she came forward and dropped abruptly to one knee.

He lunged upon her, grasping her shoulders as she started to rise. Her legs passed between his, her knees bending, her breasts rising and spreading before him. Letting him support her, she dropped her head back so that the ends of her hair touched the sand.

> Among grass,
>   briers,
> Sea oats,
>   and salt,
>
> The hair falls,
>   entangled
>
> A true tangent
>   to the earth.

His hands upon her shoulders, his legs dividing across her abdomen, he leaned over her and kissed her. Panting, he lifted his head and let her down slowly to the sand. He stepped back a moment, and then lowered himself and approached.

Kissing her thigh and groin, he continued across the gentle rounding of her abdomen until he reached her breasts — as he had moved, earlier, from the water's edge across the modulated surface of the beach, to the dunes.

As I have moved every autumn since I have played baseball over the level piney loam of the low country across the gently rolling sandhill uplands the lifting cotton and peach fields of the Piedmont the foothills the sharp friendly slopes of the Blue Ridge and into the Great Smoky Mountains . . . as every invader has ever moved from the water's edge the source across the gentleness and pushed climbed fought his way into the heart of the desirable land. . . .

He drew himself up the dampness of her body. Sweat poured from them both, mingling and dropping to the sand. They were breathing audibly, their lungs plunging at the bottom of each breath into collapse, to expand again suddenly, gasping.

   It is without movement
      that one begins,

   Without labor,
      the one searching out
         the other,

   As the fish swims,
      without movement.

         Blood falls from the hills,
          The quiet spear

         is a Spaniard
         or a Frenchman.

         Homes are fired.

> *Men gather meat from*
> *the trees,*
> *and chestnuts in*
> *the streams,*
>
> *The deer is without a mountain.*
>
> *The heart of*
> *the little squirrel*
> *Is wrapped in the skin of*
> *the bear, and*
>
> *The moon falls into the river.*
> *The little boy without feet*
>
> *runs*
> *to the middle of the sun.*
>
> *A dead man watches fire*
> *burn out the sumac*
> *on his groin.*
>
> *The river is a pumpkin.*

Sweat rolled over them, their bodies were salty and wet as though they were lying at the ocean's edge among the waves. Their eyes were watering, closed.

The sun burned intensely on Will's back. Lifting himself gently he moved to the sand. She drew his head to her side, and shielded his eyes from the sun. In a moment, he was asleep.

* * * *

When he opened his eyes, she was leaning over him, watching him. Her head, set exactly against the sun, shielding it from his eyes, seemed darker; the whites of her eyes stood out as though from negro flesh, and her hair was almost black against the brilliant sky. Her face was intent and good-humored, the lips parted slightly as before.

Stretching himself, scarcely moving, he pushed the sleep out of his muscles, as though pushing it down his arms and legs and out of his body. He raised one knee. She leaned back, touched it, ran her fingers lightly down his thigh to his hip. Shoving his elbows behind him, he raised himself, and looked down on her. She turned, resting her other cheek on his lifted chest, and their eyes met.

Hers are still watering her face warm with love and sorrow and uncertainty and fulfillment and perhaps fear her mind is divided like the tans and whites of her body divided because she wants to talk to me to secure herself with words but more than that she wants to remain silent . . . we are both renegades outcasts I cannot guess her reasons but she must know mine she must know why it is that I swim at this end of the beach this far from town and perhaps there is a certain justice in it perhaps it is right I have no claim to the beach perhaps a Santee a Yemassee an Edisto yes but did Cherokee ever hold sway east of the middle waters of the rivers. . . .

He smiled, and laughed, and gave her a gentle slap on the back. Raising herself, laughing, she sat back on her heels, her shoulders straight, her palms spread on her forelegs, so that save for the shape of her breasts she looked like a child.

Scrambling to his feet, he started out of the hollow, stretching his arm to her. She hesitated a moment, and then took his hand. They charged into the soft, steep sand on the bank of the dune, their knees pumping until they came to the top.

Still holding hands, they headed toward the ocean, walking, half running around the grass and briers, through the hollows and over the dunes. At the head of the beach, before descending to the flatness, they paused again. There was no one in sight. They remained still, gazing at the sky, the horizon clouds, the methodic rows of low breakers creeping in from the ocean. Warm ocean wind curled around them, cooling them only with its motion. Will looked down on her, on the tan legs, midriff, shoulders, arms and face, separated by two bands of white.

For an instant, she leaned her head against his shoulder.

Stepping forward, they broke the handclasp as they plunged down the face of the dune to the level of the beach. She ran as hard as she could, and Will held his pace to hers, running a few feet apart from her. As they reached the line of high tides the sand became hard packed, and the bottoms of their feet slapped against it.

The water was warm, scarcely cooler than the air. Will approached her and they ran close together, splashing each other's legs as their feet struck the foam. They ran through the first low breakers and on out. Will moved faster now, went beyond her. At the first breaker of size, he dove in, passed through it, and swam a few feet under water, close to the sand. When he came to the surface he turned, tossing the hair from his face, to see her dive in awkwardly and sit down. Catching the crest of another breaker, he rode it in, returned to her. She was laughing helplessly, splashing the water with her hands; her hair hung in wet curls against her cheeks. With both hands Will pushed the hair, then slipped his arms under shoulders and legs and picked her up. She laughed and kicked, holding firm to his neck as he turned and faced the ocean.

Walking steadily, he carried her away from the beach. At each breaker he paused and set himself, one foot diagonally behind the other, his knees flexed; he lifted her body and she buried her face in his as the wave broke. They became covered with foam as he carried her further and further, walking, pausing, setting himself, and walking again. Between breakers his eyes were set upon the dim horizon, where ocean melted into sky. She laughed like a child.

When he could carry her no further, he let her down. Her arms clung to his neck, and she clasped her legs around his. They kissed, and he held her tightly to him. They were beyond the area of the breakers; as each wave approached he gave a little spring with his feet and they floated up with it together, descending slowly on the water.

Finding that she could stand, she let herself down and they faced each other, sideways to the waves, still holding hands, floating up and descending as before.

The tide was still going out and they found themselves carried away from the beach. Separating, they started swimming in. They swam easily, close together, watching each other. She still laughed occasionally, and gulped water, but she kept pace with him. Among the breakers they started to ride on the crests, moving more rapidly. He was more skillful than she and came to the shallow breakers earlier; he sat among them and waited until she floated in. Coming together they embraced, resting as the water broke over their legs and hips.

> Waters pour two ways
>   to a joining, and
> Turn the matter.
>
> Warmness, channeled,
> Streams upon them,
>
> Upon the embracing,
>
>   and old warmth,
>   old exhaustion,
> Gulfing out of endings,
>
>   stirs.

She kissed him, grasped him firmly by an ear, by a lock of his hair. They slipped, lost balance, went under water, and came up spluttering. Breaking suddenly, she stood up and ran from him. She was laughing, exhausted. He rose and chased her, running parallel to the beach. She cut toward the ocean and he followed her. When he caught up with her, they were in the middle breakers; the water came up to his waist, and almost to her breasts. Facing the ocean, he caught her wrist, and swung her around. He lunged upon her, his legs spreading over her, and she fell back. Her head went under the ocean.

Reaching under her shoulders, he lifted her: and she came up gasping. She had swallowed deeply, and her eyes were bloodshot, the whites of them broadly exposed. Mucous and ocean poured from her nostrils. As he drew her toward him her breasts seemed to sink against her chest, and she pushed against him with real force, against his chest, neck and face. Her fingers caught in his throat; he released her suddenly and slapped her. He slapped her again.

That is an energy gathering in me without release for many years since I was a youth and lived on the reservation played the Indian ball game the energy of striking an opponent with my hand or with the stick shoving him to the ground and fighting hitting wrestling him to give up the ball then to capture it and run an energy nowhere opened in the later game. . . .

Her knees wavered and she reached toward his shoulders for support, gasping.

This is the decision the void the place where time stops the choice before an act enters the deadmarch . . .

Stepping back, he caught her hands in his. Facing the ocean, the eastern horizon, he watched her cough, struggling to approach, and held her off. They were between breakers.

> The ocean,
> foaming,
> voided by clean land . . .

Steeping back again, he let her fall, and she went down on one knee, her face dipping in and out of the water. He lunged upon her like a dog, and turned her body under his. She struggled, her knees striking his back, her fingernails digging into his arms and chest; but he discovered her throat and pressed it with both hands, under the water. Letting her do to him what damage she could, he drew his fingers tighter and tighter.

Her motion grew slower, more lethargic. Her legs were almost floating. Gradually her body became taut, her hips pushing upward against the arch of his legs, her head turned back so that it almost touched the sand.

As the head turned before,

To the earth,
>   a tangent,

Formed by her hair:

This was the beginning.

> *and with this*
> *I reclaim myself,*

Recover what is
>   *in the conch,*
>   *the gull and tern,*
>   *the long coastal sky.*

Draw back from horizons,
>   *from back breeze*
>   *over marsh grass,*

Come up from sand and briers,
Down from wing of curlew,

Out of mullet,
>   *clam shell, and*
>   *frond of palmetto.*

My parts fly back to my limbs.

Lifting himself, he jumped back from her.

It is as though she were a fish a porpoise a white whale belly-upward and dead . . .

 Her body turned over and over in the breakers, always at the surface. Her hair, following the motion, encircled her head so that her face was largely hidden; her breast and stomach and hips pushed forward on the thrust of each wave.

 Jumping back further, he moved backward toward the beach, not taking his eyes from her. The tide was still retreating, slowly pulling her away from him, and there was a cross tide, carrying her up the beach.

 Turning away for the first time, Will surveyed the land. After only a moment, he turned again to the ocean, and had to look more than once to find her. The body turned up, white and tan, in the foaming of a breaker, and then disappeared under the surface.

Facing the beach, the land, the continent, Will ran out of the ocean, to the hard sand. Bending forward, he ran hard, as he had not run in years, never in baseball; as he had not run since his youth. He ran toward the dunes, and the land beyond.

THREE

Will lay on his side on the cot, smoking quietly. His mother, who was a full-blooded Cherokee (the Scotchman had been on the father's side), sat by the table, by the oil lamp, weaving a basket. Strips of cane lay on her broad lap, and she wove them in and out among the vertical strips already attached to the base. She was a large woman, with heavy arms; she worked with great concentration, her brows knit, her eyes never lifting. Will watched her, watched her coarse fingers manipulate the cane at an unchanging pace.

He had not told her yet why he had come home. She would wait, she would not press him. The night was clear, fresh with mountain coolness; taking the air into his lungs, he felt as though he had not breathed in months. The cabin was much as he had remembered it, as it had been with only few changes since his childhood, since he could first remember. He lay still, puffing the pipe that he kept here at home, his "winter" pipe.

Lifting his eyes, he looked into her face, and it seemed also without change, seemed only to weather slowly, like the hewn logs of the cabin. She lived alone the better part of the year, but made no objection. There was a small allotment of land, farmed by relatives, and she kept chickens and a cow. She made baskets and small rugs for the tourist shops, to occupy herself. Will had sent her money from his checks now and then, but she never asked for it. Her wants appeared to be satisfied.

He could not get over the feeling, however, watching her stolid, concentrated, unexpressive face, that she must be lonely. Unlike most Indian women, she made friends poorly, and was not sociable. She avoided the dances, and the jovial obscenities that accompanied them, not because she disapproved, but because it was hard for her to join in—she had never learned how. Will's father was long dead, and a twin brother, the only other child, had died in infancy. Save for Will, she was alone in the world, and he was with her only a short portion of the year. There was one other force in her life: the church. She had been converted, and was a devout Baptist. Perhaps this was enough.

Watching her, he realized that if he was the only person close to her, the reverse was also true: she was still the only one close to him.

Perhaps when I was born my grandmother a thin leathery old woman known by many to be a witch was the midwife she stood behind my mother and held up her arms while my mother kneeled on the floor and the medicine man after giving her a decoction of the bark of the slippery elm to make the birth easier examined his beads to determine the future of the child. I was placed in a fresh deerskin and nursed on the plentiful milk of my mother's breasts together with my brother or perhaps as twins we were not raised to be normal children but witches for twenty-four days we were secluded from all visitors and denied the mother's milk but fed on connahaynee being corn parboiled beaten with a mortar and pestle returned to the pot boiled with beans and kept in a large earthen jar and at the end of twenty-four days my mother drank a decoction of the bark of the smooth sumac to make her milk flow abundantly and we were given the breast confirmed as witches. But something went wrong because my brother is dead and whatever else I can do I cannot fly through the air tunnel through the ground prepare and spoil food without touching it divine others' thoughts or walk upon sunbeams. I have wondered about my twin brother the other half of the burden of the womb what kind he was what he might have been they say he was fond of our grandmother and she of him that he used to pick up things pretty stones a flower even a dead bird and bring them to her perhaps I dominated the breast and he felt left out perhaps like the Snake Boy he left the cabin one morning without breakfast went into the woods and was gone all day returned in the evening with a pair of deer horns and went to a hut where his grandmother was waiting for him he told her he must be alone all night and she left but at daybreak she went to the hut and no boy was there but an immense green serpent with horns on its head still with human legs instead of a serpent tail. It spoke to her told her to leave and she went away and when the sun was well up it began to crawl out but it was not free of the hut until full noon it made a terrible hissing noise striking through the air like a vibrant wind reverberant and omnipresent and the people fled as it crawled among the cabins leaving a broad trail behind it until it came to the river to a deep bend in the river where it plunged in and went under the water and was never seen again. Except perhaps the grandmother who was a witch and who grieved over her grandson she went down to the river and plunged in and perhaps she saw him again. One day a man fishing saw the grandmother sitting on a large rock in the river looking as she had always looked but when she caught sight of him she jumped into the water where the Snake Boy her grandson had plunged and she was gone . . .

Will's eyes returned to his mother's hands, to the quick, restful motions of her fingers with the strips of cane . . .

As a boy I might have watched those hands dig clay from the bank of the river saw it fired in the open smoked with crushed corn cobs molded by hand decorated with paddles polished with smooth stones into pottery of chestnut-burr of frog bird fish or man. You wore beads pendants ear-ornaments and gorgets of animal teeth of bird bone of stone of pearls from the mussel of copper traded from the northern Indians of conch or other marine shells traded from Indians from the gulf or from the great eastern ocean. With my father I made arrowheads and spearheads of flint and of the antler of the deer made bows of locust and strings of the entrails of the bear blowguns of bamboo pipes of steatite and awls of bone. Gathered horse chestnuts and roots pounded them into a powder spread the powder over a lake or pond stirred it with a pole until the fish drugged by the powder floated to the surface and were gathered in baskets covered overnight against the putrefaction of the moon. I might have become an eagle hunter . . .

Will's eyes closed, but he was not asleep.

. . .called to the village in late fall or winter I would set out for the mountains engage in a vigil of prayer and fasting for four days then I would hunt and kill a deer place the body in an exposed position conceal myself and sing in an undertone to attract an eagle. When the eagle appeared I would shoot it emerge from concealment and stand over the bird say a prayer to it asserting that it was not a Cherokee that had killed it but a Spaniard! thus averting the vengeance of the eagle spirits. I would leave the bird and return to the village announcing that a snowbird had fallen thus again to mislead the eagles. Four days later when the parasites had deserted the eagle feathers the village hunters would go into the mountains they would strip the feathers and wrap them in a fresh deer skin leave the body of the deer as a sacrifice to the eagles and return to the village. The feathers would be hung in a small hut by the dance ground a dish of venison and corn set before them to satisfy their hunger also the body of a scarlet tanager. The eagle dance would be held that night and the principal chiefs would wear the feathers . . .

He opened his eyes. His mother had not changed. If she had looked at him, raised her eyes to him while his were closed, he would not know it. Save for the swishing of the strips of cane, the cabin was quiet, so that the one sound became a commotion, filled the room with the warmth of another person, of human activity. Will lifted himself part way and looked about.

The cabin was simply furnished, but it was comfortable and clean. His mother slept in the other room, on a bed that had been carved by his father before their wedding. In this room, in addition to the cot where Will slept, where he was resting now, there were two chairs and a table, and a wood stove for heat. An alcove in back, partly cut off, contained the kitchen. The floor was covered with worn linoleum. Decorations on the wall were few, and except for the religious calendar on the back of the door, they never changed from year to year. There was a small blanket that his mother had woven long ago; a bunch of dried gourds hanging in the corner; an old photograph of his mother and father together; and a newspaper reproduction of an etching of the Woolworth Building. A fishing pole stood in one corner, and a broom in another. Over the door, a rusty gun with the works broken hung on two nails. He stared at the gun for some moments.

Will became restless. Putting down the pipe, he swung his feet to the floor and stood up.

"I'll go out for a minute."

"All right."

He turned his back to her, opened the door. The swishing of the cane stopped for just a moment, and then picked up again. He didn't look back but closed the door after him, went down the steps and into the yard.

A tall cedar stood in one corner, its shape darker than the mountain and the sky. The night was clear, and the sky everywhere within the rim of mountains was filled with stars. Standing in the middle of the yard, he opened his shirt, let the cool air circulate over his chest, stomach and back.

He looked down the steep hillside, to the lights of other cabins. The sounds of dancing, chanting and drumming came to him from somewhere. A social affair, he thought; or perhaps practising for the Indian Fair. He pictured the room: small, filled with people, smoke and heat, the old folks watching the young or maybe dancing themselves, enjoying the conviviality, the excessive warmth closeted from the mountains. Beyond the cabins, in the valley bottom by the river, there was a clearing where Will had played the Indian ball game as a youth. It was still a rough game, as he had played it, but not as in the old days . . .

For ten days we would eat moderately abstain from women inure ourselves to hardship by cold plunges in the stream the night before the game we would fast and watch all night submit to scarification our skins scratched by seven splinters of turkey bone set in a frame of quill the ball ground was five hundred yards long the ball of scraped deer skin moistened stuffed with deers hair sewed with deer sinews goals marked with branches were set up at either end the object being to drive the ball through the opponent's goal the ball must be picked up by the racket and not by the hand but anything else was allowed the umpires were not called umpires but drivers. There were twelve goals to a game and if the twelve were not achieved by sunset we would fast watch another night and play the next day or as many days as might be necessary fasting and watching the intervening nights . . .

By the ball field and spotted among the cabins on the mountainside were patches of ripening corn.

Somewhere a whippoorwill was calling. *Waguli! Waguli!*

Will looked up at the mountains, at the familiar shapes and contours.

This is my home the rolling hills are my support the rim of mountains delimiting the sky the area of stars that I see is the exterior limit of my outward world. In these hills I was born and here I have lived longer than I or the dead generations before me can remember land despite what has happened to it cannot be bought cannot be owned but only poached on leased and occupied temporarily released with death like wealth which will be buried and destroyed with its owner. . .

He turned again toward the cabin, and paused. Through the glass window, he could see the deep-yellow dimness cast by the shaded oil lamp over the walls of the room, like the pleasant flame of candlelight.

I must tell her. Why else did I come back where they will look for me I must tell her why I have come home and why I must leave. I should be on the road now they will find me here but I will wait I will spend the night and get up before dawn I will go to her bed and tell her in darkness and leave at once and I will not have to see her face . . .

He paused again on the step. The night air circulating within his shirt was almost chilly. It is a sin, he thought with a smile, to sweat unnecessarily in summer.

When he opened the door, his mother didn't look up but went on weaving the strips of cane. He stepped into the room, closed the door.

The basket was almost finished. He realized that she had worked on it only to protect herself from him, to avoid the words that must be spoken. Standing before her, partly facing her, his hands in his pockets, he felt the pressure of their presences struggling to approach and avoid, denied access through tongue and eye, filling the air of the bare cabin. He shifted away, sat down on the cot. Again he watched her hands.

"Why don't you go to bed, mama," he said. "We'll talk in the morning."

She finished weaving the strip of cane, and then stopped. The room was silent.

"You work too hard," he said, laughing.

She looked up, smiled at him, and their eyes met.

"It's good to be home," he went on encouragingly.

She smiled, looked down at the basket, holding it between her hands.

"It's good to have you, Will."

She set the unfinished basket and the strips of cane on the table; leaning over, she squinted under the shade of the lamp, and turned the flame low. She rose, started toward the kitchen, and paused.

"You have enough blankets?"

"Sure, mama."

She went into the kitchen, and Will could hear her washing. He kicked off his shoes and stretched out on top of the blankets. In a moment, he heard the back door close as she went out. Lifting his arm, he shaded his eyes from the lamp, and closed them . . .

After mother's milk there is connahaynee corn is still the basic food of the Indian. In the beginning there were Kanati The Lucky Hunter and Selu The Corn Kanati brought in game and Selu washed it in the stream they had a son and the son played with a strange boy who came from the blood of the game that Selu washed in the stream Kanati Selu The Son and The Wild Boy. Selu went into a little cabin and shut the door the boys pushed out a chink of clay between the logs and watched her she stood before an empty basket she rubbed her belly and the basket was half full of corn she rubbed her armpits and the basket was full with beans The Son and The Wild Boy said we must kill her for she is a witch. Later when she saw them she looked at them and said so you know and you must kill me well when I am dead you will drag my body over the ground and sit up and watch all night wherever you drag my body corn will spring up and will be ripe before morning The Son and The Wild Boy killed her with clubs they cut off her head and put it on a stick on the house top so that Kanati would know when he returned from hunting. They dragged her body over the ground as she had told them and they watched through the night the green shoots sprang up and in the morning there was corn . . .

He heard the door close, and in a moment his mother was standing by the table, watching him. He lowered his arm.

"Do you want the light?"

"No. Blow it out."

She blew across the top of the globe, cupping her hand on the other side of it, and the flame went out. The room was in darkness. He heard the floorboards creak as she moved toward the door of her room.

"Good night."

"Good night, mama. Sleep well."

She went into her room and closed the door.

From habit Will put his arm over his eyes again, and closed them as though to sleep. But he was uneasy. He knew that he must sleep now if he was to waken early. He could not tell when he might sleep again. He lay still, tried to compose himself, but his mind moved restlessly . . .

I must fast three days drink a consecrated mixture of herbs and roots I must not rest except at night must not kill game must abstain from women a pouch at my belt filled with parched corn will be my only food . . . there is the old gun over the door but the works are broken . . . the story tells the hunters not the deer the bear wild boar or buffalo flesh to be washed in the stream but Nunyunuwi who follows the smell of human flesh the hunters turn to the man of great medicine who says seven! seven who menstruate shall be staggered unclothed in the path where Nunyunuwi comes! Nunyunuwi sees the seven naked bleeding and at the seventh oh child you are in a bad state(a virgin who has just begun to bleed) Nunyunuwi falls in vomit of blood the hunters the husbands build a great fire over Nunyunuwi who burns and crackles in late darkness from the unwashed flesh the unwashed blood the cannibal is smoke . . . Utlunta the Spear-finger may still wander in the mountains a woman monster with powers over stone she could lift great rocks and join them without mortar her skin was of rock that no weapon could wound or penetrate the stony forefinger of her right hand was of bone like an awl or a spearhead and she sang a pretty song about human liver for this was her food she would stab a hunter with the spear-finger . . .

31

He tossed about restlessly, his arm still over his eyes.

I must sleep I must sleep but if I cannot perhaps I had better go now they will come for me during the night they will think that I have come home to see my mother to eat a home-cooked meal sleep in my own cot in the cabin among the old mountains . . .

Lowering his arm, he listened. There was no sound from his mother's room. She has said her prayers and is in bed, he thought. He swung his feet to the floor, slipped them into his shoes, and waited. Among the old mountains, the night was quiet. He heard the voice of the whippoorwill.

Waguli! Waguli!

Restless as he was, it was hard for him to get up. He moved silently to his mother's door and listened. He could hear her breathing, but not the deep, regular breathing of sleep. He opened the door a little.

"Mama."

She turned over in bed. "Yes?"

He pushed the door open, and went in. His eyes were becoming accustomed to the darkness, and in the dim starlight coming through the window he made out the shape of her head on the pillow. He stood at the foot of the bed.

"Mama . . ." He hesitated, and there was a pause.

"What is it, Will?" Her voice was deep, without anxiety, and it thrust deeply into him. She has gone under me, he thought; whatever am I going to say, she has framed it so that it will be easier to say; impossible not to say.

"We had better talk now," he said, and he found his own voice more settled, from the tone of hers. "I cannot stay long." He felt a resolute hardness beginning to form in him.

"All right." She turned again, so that she lay on her back.

He approached, sat on the edge of the bed, looked down at her featureless face. Her hair was straight and black, but it had fallen loosely on the pillow in waving forms, framing her head. He looked away, looked down at his hands.

"I'm not going to play baseball any more," he said. There was silence.

"I've quit the team." Still, she said nothing, but waited for him.

"And now I've got to go. I can't stay any longer. I've got to leave, tonight." He looked up, and for the first time he was able to see the glint of her eyes. "I may not see you again."

She turned away, gazed through the window at the starlight. There was a long silence. As though it were an object whose approach he could watch, a sound to be seen rather than heard, he became aware of gentle sobbing, like the breaking of low waves on the beach. Her heavy arm came from under the covers, and without waiting for it he leaned toward her, let her hand settle on the back of his neck. He put his head beside hers on the pillow . . .

When the warrior is taken prisoner he is tied by a long grape vine to a stake a firebrand is placed on the stake the warrior sings recounts his triumphs in battle while the women who are called Pretty Women *rush at him with lighted brands . . . The warrior fights back and when his tender parts become burned the women pause pour cold water over him allow him to recover then they start again if he is brave he resists defies boasts sings to the end. When he falls they scalp him amputate all exterior parts the women singing with joy during the torture while the men watch. What she is beginning to offer me what I am submitting to willingly what I have come home at the risk of my life to receive from her hands is scarcely more sufferable . . .*

Withdrawing her other arm from the covers, she placed a hand on either side of his head and lifted it, held it above hers. She stared into his eyes, and he into hers.

"What have you done, Will?"

"I have killed..." She held him, the sobs withheld. He had not finished, and she would not release him until he had.

"I killed a woman."

She held him a moment longer, then her hands dropped, and his head wavered a moment, discovered its own support. Her broad arms lay loosely on the covers, and she turned again to the starlight. Her breath came shortly: she was almost gasping. Suddenly, she cast an arm around his neck and drew him toward her again, so that his face was buried against hers...

Now I have crossed her twice taken from her the sole survivor of her love and motherhood and committed the bitterest violence in her constellation of meekness the Christian belief thou shalt not kill. As nearly as any force of and within life can approach her destruction I have approached it now...

Held tight against his mother's face, he thought back, bitterly and sadly, to the church of his youth. He remembered the part-singing of hymns by the Indian voices, and he remembered the look of open, profound sadness that the hymns, sung in Cherokee tongue, brought to the faces of Indian women. He remembered holding his mother's hand or dress, standing beside her, a mountain of strength and sadness. He remembered hating the sadness in her eyes, hating the hymns.

He held himself against her face, made no effort to struggle against the firm grip of her arm. She wept heavily, bitterly.

She does not blame me that would be easy to accept an anger from which we would both recover but she blames herself. She is remembering Will the intractable aberrant child and recognizes in me as she has many times before her own nature remote and difficult of access. We are of one nature the seed is the same we have become different only as an accident of exterior event . . .

Tears poured from her eyes, struggled for passage between their cheeks. When he felt them on his face, salty and burning, he lifted himself, gently but forcefully. Again their eyes met. He watched her broad, ruddy face swollen with tears, her high cheekbones, the dishevelled hair on the pillow, the eyes narrowed and scarcely open.

The resoluteness that had begun to form earlier became harder within him. One of the tears from her face slipped down his own cheek and into the corner of his mouth. He closed his lips, drew them together.

Except for the word for salt and the word for water the Cherokee tongue is a lipless tongue spoken with the lips parted not clapping together not breaking into fractions the flow of thought but allowing it like the constant pouring of the streams and rivers the changeless motion out of the Smokies out of the great underworld whose only access is at the streams' heads. But in the word salt and the word water in salt water the lips draw together and become tight as tight and narrow as the lips of the blue-eyed Scotchman . . .

"I must go," he said.

His mother said nothing, but her weeping became gentler.

Tsulkalu the Slant-Eyed Giant came into the village and took a young virgin for wife he never showed himself but came after dark to lie with the girl and left before dawn he left meat for the girl and her mother and the mother was glad. One night he reached into the stream where the girl had bathed at the unclean time of month and he brought forth a baby daughter Tsulkalu took his wife and child and left for the mountains the girl's brother followed them and found places where there had been a childbirth and where the children had played he came to a cave in the mountains where many people were dancing his sister came out and spoke to him. Tsulkalu did not come but he promised to appear in the village if the people would fast for seven days and seven nights the people gathered in the council house but there was a stranger with them who slipped out at night and broke the fast at the end of the seventh night the people heard a roar approaching from the mountains like thunder or a rock-slide the roar became louder and louder the stranger screamed and ran out of the council house the sound stopped. Then it started again and slowly disappeared into the mountains and Tsulkalu was never seen . . .

He withdrew from her, still sitting on the bed.

"I'm going into the mountains," he said; "and across them. I'll head west."

"You'll need food . . ."

"Don't worry."

". . . and money . . ."

"I have some . . ."

"The loose brick in the chimney . . . I've saved the money you sent me."

"No, mama . . ."

"Take it!" Her tone was deep again, informed with tragedy, subverting and holding their whole relation. She turned away from him, gazed again at the starlight.

"All right."

A light flashed across the window. She must have seen it, but she made no motion. Will sprang to his feet.

He went to the other room, to a front window. A disc of light was approaching over the rough ground of the yard. He could not see the flashlight or the figure that held it; only the bright circle following the path to the cabin. In three leaps he was across the cabin and into the kitchen, to a back window. Another circle was fixed on the grass, white, motionless. He turned, slowly, walked back to the front room. He made no motion for the loose brick in the chimney. Instead, he went to the cot, picked up his jacket, and held it over his arm. He remained still.

His mother continued to sob softly. Like the persistence of the waves, he thought. There was muffled conversation outdoors, and the light swept once across the front of the cabin; Will was out of range as it flashed through the window. Footsteps approached, and there was heavy knocking on the door. Then silence. Will was motionless.

"Come on out, Smoky."

Separated from him by the logs of the cabin, the words were muffled, inchoate. There was a pause.

"You'd better come, boy. We know you're there."

The voice was paternal, harsh only with the nature of its purpose, not of the man. Again there was silence, and a long pause. Even the sobbing of Will's mother had quieted. The door was kicked open, swung into the room, and the flashlight, backed by two figures, entered the opening. Will was at one side, and a moment passed before the light discovered him.

"All right, boy."

FOUR

At a fork in the path he stopped, caught his breath. His clothes were still wet in the night air, clinging to him, making him cold while he was still sweating. His shoulder throbbed regularly, the pain becoming more intense where the bullet lodged in it. He had no idea how long he'd been walking. He looked at the sky, recalled that he had once been able to tell time by the appearance of the stars, but had forgotten. Breathing more easily, he turned to the path that followed the stream, and went forward.

Again he walked and climbed for a long time, moving at a steady pace. The pain spread into his chest and part way down his arm. The area felt as though it were swelling. At a point where the path touched the edge of the stream, he stopped, was still, recovering his breath. For the first time, he looked at the wound. The jacket must have been thrown open at the time, for the bullet had escaped it, but had torn a hole in his shirt. Streaks of blood, partly dried, had gone down the arm and front of the shirt. He realized that he couldn't repair the hole, but would have to wash out the blood; and the wound should be washed and covered. He must find a place where he could stop for the night and sleep, where he could build a fire to keep war, and dry his clothes. His mind, accelerated in the pace of his flight, had to be caught and slowed, like his breathing:since the shooting, he had formed no useful plan.

He looked at the sky again. The pattern of stars, largely hidden by the pines, was of no help. He knew however that he was well into the mountains, and he guessed the hour at after midnight. Lowering his eyes, he discovered and immediately remembered a low ridge, descending from the higher mountains, diverting the flow of the stream around its point as it fell to an end. He recalled the far side, the western side of the ridge, and realized that it offered a safe location for a fire and for the night. Matches were in his jacket pocket, they were safe and dry. Firewood could be found.

His head felt cloudy, and he thought he would become dizzy; but he remained still, and recovered himself, He knew that he was feverish. Taking off his jacket, putting it on the ground, he carefully removed the shirt. Shreds of it were caught in the dried blood, and the wound started to bleed again as he tore it away.

He soaked the shirt in the stream, and spread it over a bare rock. With sand from the edge of the water he scrubbed the stains, holding the shirt with the hand of the wounded arm. After the second rinse, the blood was gone and a faint yellow stain remained: it was the best he could do. Carrying the shirt and jacket, he made his way along the edge of the stream and around the bend.

The far side of the ridge was sheer rock, like a cliff. A short distance from the stream there was an indentation where the rock was partly hollowed. It was not a cave, but the cliff beetled overhead and gave protection: the light of a fire would not be seen from the east.

Spreading the shirt on a rock he went out for firewood. With dry leaves and pine needles for kindling, he built a fire and ignited it, crouched before it, helped the flames to catch, and felt their first warmth. The night air was cold, and penetrated as soon as he stopped moving. The wounded arm hung limply at his side.

His head clouded again and he felt the approaching vertigo. He stood up, tried to secure himself, collect his balance, realized that he would have to dress the wound quickly if it were to be done, for he needed rest. Walking uncertainly, guiding himself along the cliff, he returned to the stream and crouched at the edge, shivering with cold and fever.

He soaked his handkerchief in the water, and began to wash the wound. It was swollen and the pain was intense . . .

The stream the mountain stream emerging at its head from the underworld is purifying and health-giving its flow is eternal and is therefore sacred as the source of life its waters on the wound are not a specific but they are the best I can do. To be right I should sing the formula in the middle of the rocks in the middle of the earth in the middle of the woods in the middle of the water and I would say now then! in the centre you are staying Brown Dog now you have come to let your path down you have come to halt in the middle of the spot where the blood is spouting now it has become your saliva relief has been caused at once now then! and I would chew on the bark of the hickory and through a hollow buzzard quill cut off at both ends I would blow the hickory and saliva upon the wound if a buzzard quill were not available the hollow stalk of the Gerardia would suffice but the buzzard in his foulness has great power over the foulness of infection. In addition I would pluck a ginseng root in the woods dropping a bead in the hole in payment for it and the ginseng would cure the vertigo I would make a poultice of the bark of the Tag Alder to soothe the swelling and a decoction of Wild Cherry bark boiled over the fire and drunk as tea would reduce by fever. But if I am feverish if I am sick there may be more than the wound as a cause the animals and insects that wittingly or unwittingly I have abused are striking the illness into me or I am longing for association with the departed with the spirit of some beloved my father or my brother who has gone to the Darkening Land in the West and who longs for me as I for him who exerts himself upon me to cause me through illness and death to join him mooning over the dead is not healthy . .

When the wound was clean he rinsed the handkerchief, soaked it again, and folded it double. He draped it over his shoulder so that it rested against the opening. The bleeding had stopped.

He returned, chattering with cold and fever, and added wood to the fire, sat as close to it as he could. Arranging his jacket as a pillow he lay down, moving carefully so as not to disturb the handkerchief. His body ached with fatigue, and his shoulder became numb.

With the rock rising around him, the fire sheltering him from the night, he felt truly as though he were in a cave.

The Cherokee are people who live in caves the original Chalaqué the word used by the Choctaws the Indians of the Gulf Coast who met De Soto in Florida and who told him of us called us Chalaqué the people who come out of caves . . .

His eyes closed, and at once visions of the shooting, and all that led up to it flashed into his mind. He recalled leaving the cabin, and walking single file down the road, toward the officers' car. He recalled jerking the gun out of the holster of the man in front of him, and shooting while he scrambled over the roadbank. He recalled the groaning, cursing figures lying on the road, the flashlights departed from their hands. His head began to twist back and forth, slowly, on the jacket, like the body of the wounded officer rolling in the gravel. His lips were dry, his mouth open. He became delirious with fever . . .

I am dreaming I am dreaming if I dream of birds I will go insane if I dream of wrestling with a fat women or having sexual relations with my mother I will be stricken with rheumatism will be unable to move through the mountains if I dream of bees and wasps I will go blind. If I dream if I have a vision of the Darkening Land in the West it will mean that I am about to die the medicine man will attempt the cure for apoplexy and failing in that my family will serve me a square meal as square as I can eat to carry me on my journey death being a movement in space not in time no other preparations will be made lest they betray anxiety and when I die a relative will straighten the legs the arms place the hands on the abdomen tie a white kerchief around the head and chin to hold the lips together a friend not a relative will wash the body dress it in fine clothes given for the purpose and the body will be kept in the house for several days to be viewed by family and friends will be watched over at night protected against witches against Utlunta the Spear-finger who might steal the fresh-dead liver or against the Raven Mocker. The grave will be dug the body will be placed in the coffin will be avoided by medicine men and pregnant women whose business is life and not death the friends and family will pass in a circle around the coffin for a last look at the face and the coffin will be covered will be lowered into the grave with the head inclining westward toward the Darkening Land the grave will be filled and the burial finished. Seven days after death a dance will be held to speed the dead to divert the immediate relatives unlimber them freshen them with the feeling of life . . .

He slept. He must have slept. Once during the night, during the darkness, he awoke. The fire had burned low and he was chilly, but his head was clear. The fever had burned partly out of him, and the throbbing in his shoulder had changed to a dull, steady ache. The woods, the mountains were silent. He lay still, looked up, past the overhanging rock, through the pine tops to the sky . . .

The hunters were camping in the mountains one night when they saw two lights moving along a distant ridge they watched and wondered they saw them the next night and the next on the third morning they crossed to the ridge they found two creatures round and large with fine gray fur and little heads like those of terrapins when the breeze played upon the fur showers of sparks flew out the hunters kept them several days at night they would grow bright and shine by day they were balls of gray fur except when the wind stirred and the sparks flew out they were quiet and no one thought of their trying to escape but on the seventh night they rose from the ground like balls of fire above the tree tops climbing higher and higher until they were only bright points the hunters then knew they were stars . .

Again he slept. When he woke, the birds were singing, and the gray dawn had crept over the ridge into the valley. The pines were motionless in the still air.

The fire had gone out and he was stiff with cold, with the clotted pain in his shoulder. He lay still for a moment, not shivering, but afraid to move. The night came back to him: confession, capture, shooting and escape; delirium and dreams, expulsion of fever.

All that is in back of me if not in the lowlands at least in the foothills to the east parted from me by the impenetrable rock at my back. I bear the wound of it in my shoulder and the tears of my mother in my heart but rock is harder the rock is a shell projecting me westward and although I have not crossed the highest ridge the divide between east and west I am facing it I will cross it and descend westward I will follow the half-blood Sequoyah who tamed the wild animal of language who wrote the word who crossed the Great River in search of his Cherokee brother to teach him the word went west and then south into Mexico . . .

Pulling back his arms, he lifted himself slowly. His muscles were strained and rigid, cracking like old leather, and the early, sharp pains of the bullet wound revived, shooting down his arm and side. The handkerchief on his shoulder had dried, was stuck to the wound. He walked slowly to the stream and poured water on the handkerchief until it came loose. Then he soaked it and replaced it as before. He returned and built a fire. There was still no sunlight, only the gray chilly dawn. The leaves ignited quickly and the flames came up; he crouched before them, hungry for warmth. His shirt was dry, and he held it to the flames for a moment, then slipped it carefully over his wounded shoulder and put it on. He put on the jacket, and felt warmer.

Taking his wallet from his jacket, he removed all the contents except money. One by one he slipped the various cards and papers into the fire: social security, driver's license, draft card, certificate of award from a Rotary Club for being a twenty-game winner . . .

This is the end this is the finish never again will I look to the east . . .

He stood up, still gazing at the fire. The woods were loud and confused with birdsong. Stepping forward, he trampled on the fire, lifting his feet only slightly, shuffling through it until it was out. He stepped back and watched to make sure that no sparks were left;

then he turned and headed for the stream.

I am hungry it will be a long time before I will dare approach a highway to buy beg or even steal food first I must get across the ridge and into Tennessee but I am hungry I must have something before then perhaps soup from the roots of the greenbrier bear rib barbecued on a hickory stick served with poke leaf and rattlesnake meat also chestnut bread and wild honey spicewood tea to drink and for dessert opossum grapes or persimmons with hickory nuts. But not like Tsali and the others I am a fugitive in the mountains there are no nuts or acorns in summer I will have only berries and bark . . .

He forded the stream and moved away from it, headed diagonally up the wall of the valley. The going was rough, almost impossible through a tangle of undergrowth, the rhododendron and laurel, but he drove himself forward at an unchanging pace, as he had the night before. The shoulder throbbed in every movement of flesh.

The sun came up, striking his back as he retreated from it. He stopped at a waterfall, to drink; the grass was thick and damp, and maidenhair ferns were uncurling. Nearby he found blackberries, and he picked them and ate.

He pushed on. The sun was getting hot, and he took off his jacket, tied it around his waist. He began to hear an occasional car or truck, and knew that he was approaching the highway. He would have to cross it. Climbing steeply, he caught a glimpse of it, of the cut in the rock where it passed. He waited beside a tree while a heavy tractor-trailer swing around the curve, heading downward to North Carolina. Coming closer, he had to crawl on hands and knees, the bank was steep. At the edge of the paving, he ducked behind shrubbery as a car approached. He watched it pass: a new car filled with tourists and laden on top, sides and back with luggage, camping equipment, fishing rods, camera tripods, etc. When it had gone, he lay still and listened. There was no other sound. Scrambling to the pavement, he ran across and ducked into the thick woods on the other side. He was out of sight.

Still he climbed, moving toward the ridge, toward a remote part of the mountains. He followed the stream beds where possible, to avoid the impenetrable tangles of undergrowth. Crossing a well-marked path, coming to it suddenly, without warning, he paused, listened, but there was no sound: he hastened into the woods beyond.

The sun climbed steadily, as though in extension of his own climbing. His shirt and handkerchief became drenched in sweat, but he didn't slow down or pause. So long as he climbed, so long as the ridge lay ahead of him, he was not tired.

In the high exposed areas, many of the pines were dead and rotting away, victims of blight. Some were still standing, the branches jagged and naked, others had fallen, the great trunks lying gray and without bark on the mountainsides. Will climbed over or crawled under them, staying as much as possible under the living trees.

As the morning grew older the birds retired and the woods became quiet. Only the junco fluttered persistently in the mountain ash.

At midday with the sun overhead, he reached the crest, the border of North Carolina and Tennessee, the divide between eastern and western Appalachian slopes, between Atlantic and Mississippi waters. There was a small clearing, an outcropping of rock. He approached, staying under the trees to avoid the sweeping eyes of binoculars, and looked out. A wide view of mountains met his eyes, of the Balsam range and others to the east and south. In the blue smoke of midday they seemed like soft waves, motionless and floating. Forested whorls, star whirls and trowel scoops, gigantic and gentle, altered the surface. Cradled among them was Fontana Lake, the waters of the Little Tennessee dammed and impounded. As he gazed at it, at the sparkling blue, Will suddenly became tired. His legs ached, his shoulder pained him and his eyes filled with tears of fatigue. He thought he would become ill again if he could not eat and rest . . .

In the wildest depths of the Great Smokies lies the enchanted lake of Atagahi no one has seen it for the way is so difficult that only the animals can approach should a hunter come near he would know of it by the whirring of thousands of wild ducks and pigeons but he would not see it without praying and fasting and watching through the night floating lilies grow in its purple waters it is fed by springs spouting from the high cliffs around it Atagahi is the medicine lake of the birds and animals when a bear is wounded by the hunters he makes his way through the woods to the lake and plunges in when he comes out upon the other side the wounds are healed for this reason the animals keep the lake invisible to the hunters . . .

Turning from the lake and mountains, Will entered the woods and crossed the ridge, moving west.

FIVE

and the noble hidalgos sold their estates gave up their incomes from land and church crowded into Seville to join Hernando de Soto fresh from the conquest of Peru now Governor of the Island of Cuba and Adelantado of Florida possessed of a fortune in Inca gold to be traded for the conquest of Florida. There was not space on the ships some gentlemen were left on the docks their luggage around them their goods and estates sold six hundred were chosen by the Governor and more than two hundred of the finest Spanish horses great festivities were held the trumpets sounded artillery blasted as the seven ships sailed out of the harbor. The fleet paused in the Canary Islands for bread and wine and meat and sailed out again arrived in Santiago de Cuba where the party divided some traveled by land others by sea to the port of Havana. Two months the Governor spent in final preparations in settling the affairs of his island arranging a home for his bride the Donna Isabella on a Sunday in the warm Caribbean spring the fleet set sail once more quitting the Island for the vast indeterminate continent known only as Florida. For twelve days the ships sailed the blue waters of the Gulf and on Friday the Thirtieth Day of May in the Year of Our Lord Fifteen Hundred and Thirty-Nine the first landing was made on the banks of a river in celebration whereof the place was named Puerto del Espiritu Santo . . .

"My name's Ferd. Hop in."

Will was standing on U.S. 80, west of Jackson, Mississippi, when a truck slowed for him. He ran to catch up with it, and he was out of breath. When the driver put out his hand to him, accompanying the greeting, Will grasped it like a handle to pull himself up. The driver responded, gripping firmly and pulling. The muscle in the wounded shoulder wrenched as Will swung into the cab, and sharp pains went down his arm. He settled back in his seat and closed the door with his left hand.

"Where you bound?"

"West," said Will. He was still breathing hard, his arm resting limply in his lap. "Texas."

"Good. I'm heading for Dallas."

The driver glanced in the mirror and then concentrated on the road, as he started forward. It was a heavy truck, with extra gears and a roaring, grinding motor. The effort of acceleration suggested a full load. Will shifted his feet among a mass of tools, jacks, rags, etc. Over the windshield, and on the side and back walls between the windows, were snapshots of girls; a small calender featuring a nude; a couple of kupie dolls; and business cards of various drive-ins, restaurants, garages, etc.

Will glanced at Ferd. He was a slender, blue-eyed man of perhaps thirty, his face tense and alert. His eyes remained fixed on the road. Will turned away and looked out the window.

"Cigarette?"

When he looked back, Ferd was holding the pack, offering them.

"Thanks."

"Light one for me."

Will took two from the pack, waited for the matches that followed. He lit the cigarettes, his right hand trembling a little, and handed one to Ferd, together with the matches.

The first drag of smoke felt good and Will inhaled deeply, blowing it out with force. He leaned back, resting his head on the worn leather, and inhaled again. The cab became filled with the pleasant smoke. Ferd held his cigarette tightly between his lips, smoking without removing it.

"My name's Joe," Will said.

Ferd nodded without turning, and they drove on.

The Indians approached playing flutes as a sign of peaceful intentions the Cacique spoke VERY HIGH POWERFUL AND GOOD MASTER the things that seldom happen bring astonishment think then what must be the effect on me and mine the sight of you and your people whom we have at no time seen astride the fierce brutes your horses entering with such speed and fury into my country that we had no tidings of your coming things so altogether new as to strike awe and terror to our hearts which it was not nature to resist so that we should receive you with the sobriety due to so kingly and famous a lord trusting to your greatness and personal qualities I hope no fault will be found in me and that I shall rather receive favours of which one is that with my person my country and my vassals you will do as with your own things and another that you tell me who you are whence you come whither you go and what it is you seek that I may the better serve you. De Soto thanked him and replied that he was the child of the Sun that he came from the land of the Sun that he was traveling in search of treasure he erected a great wooden cross on the mound in the town-yard told the Indians it was put there to commemorate the suffering of Christ who was God and man that He had created the skies and the earth and had suffered for the salvation of all and therefore they should revere that sign and they the Indians showed by their manner that they would. Whereupon as in every territory the Spaniards crossed the Cacique was taken prisoner slaves were demanded put in chains and iron collars to carry the burdens trinkets and mirrors were traded to the men for their women and the Christians lived off the crops and stores of the land beat the maize with mortar and pestle sifted it through their coats of armour baked it in clay dishes over fires after the manner of Indians. Throughout the summer they pushed through the wilds and tangles of the Florida peninsula changing Cacique and slaves and women at the border of each territory the Indians soon learned to give them false promises of gold and maize in the land beyond in order to be rid of them . . .

Ferd pushed the truck into high gear and set it at a steady fifty miles an hour. The highway passed over rolling hills and level farm land, and the speedometer never varied more than a mile or two either side of fifty. He flicked his head sharply, and the ashes from his cigarette fell between the spokes of the steering wheel to the floor.

Will continued to lean back, his head on the leather, his eyes lazily watching the road. The cigarette, that had at first relieved his hunger and exhaustion, now intensified them. He let it burn down by itself, and threw it out the window.

For twelve days he had slept only an hour or two at a time, in woods and fields, beside streams. He had lived on corn and other vegetables taken at night from fields and gardens and eaten raw, and what few berries he could find in the woods. He had not been cold, it was summer and he was out of the mountains; but he had walked and walked, day and night, had walked through his shoes and was wearing a pair that he had taken from the feet of a drunk he had found asleep in a ditch. Until now he had hitch-hiked only occasionally, for short rides on back roads. This was the first time he had dared a main highway. He was gambling on a long haul, and apparently had won. Always, as he walked or rode, or tried to sleep, there was the dull ache in his shoulder. He had spent some of his little cash at a general store for needle and thread, and had sewed the bullet hole in his shirt. But he still wore the jacket although it was late morning and the day was hot and humid.

The roar of the motor became a steady drone. He could feel

himself becoming drowsy, beginning to sink, as though into the enormous emptiness of his stomach. He held his eyes open with an effort. If I grit my teeth, he thought; imagine that the air filtering between them is a thin solid, that I am holding myself to it like an acrobat hanging by his teeth; or like a drowning man, struggling to hold mouth and nose above the surface . . .

. . . Until in one town still in the peninsula of Florida the Indians planned an attack to release the captured Cacique but the Spaniards attacked first drove the Indians into a lake the Indians swam out beyond range of the crossbow and harquebus refused to surrender darkness fell the Indians were treading deep water in the middle of the lake some swam in silently waterlilies covering their heads and tried to scramble out but De Soto's cavalry encircling the lake discovered them plunged into the water to the horses' breasts drove the Indians back to the middle of the lake some surrendered exhausted and cold but at dawn twelve were still treading water others swam out and brought them in for their endurance they were tied to a stake and shot . . .

"Do you see that one?"

Ferd was pointing to one of the snapshots over the windshield. Will stirred himself and looked at head and shoulders of a pretty girl, with hard, vigorous face.

"Used to be my girl friend." He turned quickly to Will, and his blue eye winked. "Small town in Georgia. That was when I was hauling hardware out of Augusta. Used to run down to spend the night." Again he turned quickly, his face bright with pleasure.

"Nine brothers and thirteen sisters," he went on, shouting above the drone of the motor. "One of them had epilepsy. Some in the navy, three in marines, a couple of wacs. One worked a carnival, another studying to be a sky pilot. Some of the girls married off and left town, didn't even know where they were. And could she fight! Umh!"

He leaned over the steering wheel, gripping it strenuously for emphasis.

"First time we went out she blacked my eyes. Next time, we were fooling around in the front parlor and she hit me with a solid brass lamp!"

Felled pines across the stream bound them with withes fought off the Indians as they crossed and entered the town that the Indians had burned before flight this being Wednesday of Saint Francis . . .

"But I tamed her. Man, I tamed her!" He sat back, spreading his elbows. "One of her brothers that was away in service had a guitar that he kept home, and that's one box I can really play. I used to take her back by the barbecue and play for her, and she'd sing. Sometimes we'd both sing, with me on the harmony. We'd eat hamburgers on corn bread—did you every try it? Singing like that, eating outdoors on a summer night, twanging the guitar real slow, she'd go all soft. After that it was easy. I'd take her out to a cabin, or maybe we'd go up to Augusta, to a hotel. She was really built, you can't tell from that." He shook his hand deprecatingly at the photograph.

Maize pumpkin bean and plum with rabbit opossum turkey and partridge the autumn harvest of a continent and the Spaniards pushed northward and eastward until they reached Cofitachiqui the name of a town a territory and of the lovely Cacica who ruled them. The town lay across a river and the Cacica came out to greet the Spaniards she was carried in a litter to the water's edge stepped into a magnificent canoe reclined in the stern on mats and cushions under an awning while her vassals paddled her across the stream accompanied by her retinue of consorts in lesser canoes. She greeted De Soto took a string of pearls from her throat with her own hands dropped them over his head her men ferried the Christians across the river and she gave them decorated deer skins and cloaks of thread made from the bark of the mulberry tree others of white gray vermilion and yellow feathers she gave them turkeys to eat noting their interest in pearls she graciously led them to a sepulchre from which they took several hundred pounds. So fine the pearls so abundant the food so generous the Cacica many of the men wanted to settle to divide the land among themselves but De Soto remembered the Andes the Inca the gold. He took the lovely lady prisoner obtained slaves and pushed northwestward to the great mountains . . .

"That was right after the war, when hardware was scarce. Fellow with a truck could make a good living, provided he could find it. I got in with this operator in Augusta, strictly black market. I was hauling back up to Asheville and around there. That's my home."

He turned to the window and spat out the cigarette, that had burned almost to his lips. He was silent for a while, his eyes bright and alert as he watched the road.

"When hardware began to get easy I had to give it up. It was then my luck started going sour. I'd just bought a new semi—tractor-trailer, you know?—and she was a beauty. Brand new, all aluminum. Cost me two hundred and fifty for the tags alone. Had to mortgage the house to get her. Here."

He took down another snapshot and put it into Will's hands. It showed a young woman seated on the porch of a house, holding a baby in her arms.

"That's the wife. Finest little chick in the world. I wouldn't take a purty for her. And you see that kid? He's four years old now. Smart as a whip. Last Christmas I gave him a jig-saw puzzle, a map of the country, with a piece for every state, you know? The wife said it was too smart for him, I should have saved it. Well, I didn't give him a bit of help, I just set it down on the floor in front of him and damned if he didn't figure it all out by himself. Now he can put it together in five minutes. What I mean, smart. We got another one on the way now. That's the house, you can see a little of it there, the one that's got the mortgage on it."

Will nodded and handed him the snapshot. He replaced it over the windshield.

"I got a deal going between Asheville and Atlanta, with this new semi. Two or three trips a week, regular. Nice business. Well, one morning, it was winter, and I set out of Asheville about four or five o'clock, loaded down with beer. I got out beyond the mountains the other side of the Gap. It's nice and straight going up, you know, but down the other side it's just one hairpin after another. It was daylight by then, but raining and foggy, and I was driving with lights. I got on one of them turns and the brakes give out. The pedal went down to the floor like I was stepping on air. Brand new truck, didn't have two thousand on her by then! I wrenched that wheel one way and the other, curled back and forth like a damn snake. I cut into the bank on the inside, took a chunk out of it and heaved back on the road. I made the curve all right, but I wasn't stopped, not by a long shot. I wasn't hardly slowed. There was a straight piece ahead, not long, but straight down, with another hairpin at the end. I snaked her back and forth and I could feel that beer swinging behind me like I was swinging the whole mountain by the tail. I shoved her out of gear and jammed her into second, nearly broke my arm. That slowed her some, but not enough. By the time I got to the hairpin I knew we couldn't make it. She was going to pitch off and I was going to pitch with her. I opened the door and half hung on it, watching. My foot was still sitting on that damn fool brake pedal out of habit, and I was snaking the wheel. The bank was so steep that it wasn't until we come right up on it that I could see over. Cleared all the way, not a tree or nothing, two or three hundred feet down to the stream bed. Right at the edge of the road, when the front wheels took off, I jumped clear. It wasn't until I was half out of the truck and I couldn't have done nothing about it nohow that I saw where I was heading—a hunk of rock sticking up straight out of the bushes. I missed it all except my right leg and that got smashed against it and tore up all to pieces. Holes and gashes and bones sticking out. I mean, it was a mess!

"I didn't black out. I watched that tractor break loose and roll over and over; I watched that pretty aluminum trailer shear open like it was made out of paper. The two of them rolled down and came together again by the stream bed, where they caught fire. I just lay back and didn't look no more. And you know that damned white trash, they must have smelled it for six counties around: they started coming out of the woods and picking up the beer bottles that wasn't broke . . ."

...But they arrived in the mountains of the Chalaque in late spring and there was little maize because the winter stores were gone and the summer crops had not come in nevertheless they ate dogs. The captive Cacica Cofitachiqui led them a merry chase in search of gold through the blue-hazed ridges and smoke-blue mountains and quietly escaped taking with her a box of the finest pearls and a handsome Negro slave to share the doeskin mats to idle the hours of night down by the river . . .

"I didn't lay there long. The bank was all tore up where we'd gone off, and the truck was lit up like a forest fire. Couple of fellows in a pickup stopped and I hollered to them. They came over and picked me up, carried me into their truck, with the leg dangling like a half butchered ham, and them afraid to touch it. They hauled me into a clinic in this small town, the trap bouncing like a buckboard, me stretched out in back. The doctor wasn't there, it was too early, and the nurse didn't much know what to do. I was talking wild, I guess, and cussing, and she got kind of hysterical and pumped me full of dope to cut the edge out of my tongue. The doctor came and I still hadn't gone out. He looked at the leg and then he gave me a look that told me he was fixing to use the hatchet. I sat up and cussed him out something awful, told him I'd as soon let him have my neck. He talked back and I just talked louder. God knows what I said but I pitched him a mean fit. They packed me into an ambulance and headed for Asheville and me still babbling and carrying on. Somewhere on the road I blacked out, and I didn't know nothing for a day and a night . . ."

Southward and westward the Spaniards turned moving down the southern passes of the mountains to the level land the rivers pouring to the Gulf of New Spain they came to Taszaluza where a giant Cacique sat in a litter attended by his chiefs by a slave who fanned the flies from him he watched the Spaniards put on a show jousting running the horses and said nothing when De Soto demanded food and slaves he replied that he was accustomed to having others serve him and was put in chains. He sent word to Mauvila another of his towns to gather the warriors and told his captors their desires would be satisfied in Mauvila the Spaniards carried him thence a stockaded town stakes driven in the ground interlaced with withes covered inside and out with clay De Soto and others entered by way of graciousness and were entertained by women who danced for them and the attack began. The Spaniards were wounded but save only a priest and a friar they escaped the stockade in the confusion the slaves bearing the Christian possessions entered struck off their iron collars and joined the attack. The wounded Governor reformed the cavalry approached the stockade the fighting was bitter and bloody slowly hour after hour the horsemen came closer until brands thrown over the wall fired the huts and the Christians entered the last confusion fighting within the stockade choked with thatch of huts in smoke and flame and the rampage of horses with Indians dead and burned and wounded fighting falling and clustering was bloodiest of all the mounted Spaniards shot and slashed and fired until the natives were exterminated until the last warrior hung himself from a tree to escape surrender. The Spaniards withdrew to the open field beyond the smoldering huts and lay down to nurse their wounds to count their losses. Indians lay dead by thousands the Spaniards had lost perhaps a hundred with hundreds wounded many of the best horses killed and wounded. All the possessions the clothes the pearls of Cofitachiqui were lost. The priest and friar trapped within the village had been rescued were safe this was a blessing but the ornaments for the saying of mass the sacramental cups the moulds for making wafers the wine were gone. Worst of all worse than the loss of cloak horse or brother the precious wheat flour cherished from Spain was destroyed henceforth the Christians would partake of His body with no wine with wafers crudely fashioned of the profane maize. The fighters bemoaned their fate dressed their wounds with fat from the bodies of the dead Indians . . .

"When I come to I was in a ward in the hospital. I cussed out the first nurse I saw until she told me I still had my leg. She told me I hadn't ought to have had it, that any other doctor in Buncombe County would have whacked it off, but this fellow I happened to get was a wizard and he'd put it back together again. They still didn't know, they have to wait until the bones set. So there was nothing for me to do but lay there week after week, counting up my debts and watching the pus pour out of the holes."

Ferd paused, and Will turned to the window, looked over the level Mississippi farmland, negro and white, spreading northward. The weather was hot and oppressive, and a bank of dark clouds threatened over them. Ferd remained silent, and Will became disturbed. He realized that he had come to depend on the driver's story to support the exhausted thread of his own conciousness.

"The leg doesn't bother you now?" he asked.

"Not a bit," Ferd replied at once, as though he had been waiting for Will to ask him. "I get a twinge now and then, but I can do just about anything with it I could before. The bones set just as pretty as you could wish, and they stuck me full of penicillin until it was coming out of my ears. That dried up the pus and closed the holes. After six weeks I crawled out on crutches. It took another month at home, just laying around doing nothing. Cigarette?"

"I'll light one for you."

Will performed the service for Ferd and handed him the lighted cigarette.

"Thanks. So there I was. Debts on the house, the doc and the hospital. And no truck. Time that wreck stopped burning, they hauled it out and sold it for junk. Had to bulldoze a road down there to get it out. The insurance paid off, but the finance comapny got most of that. So I put myself in hock again and bought this trap. I figured if I didn't have some kind of truck, I never would get out of the hole."

He turned to emphasize the point with an inquiring look, and Will nodded. Again there was silence, as Ferd gazed at the road. Will could feel himself sinking, drowsily.

"What are you hauling?" he asked, shifting his position.

"Peaches. Spartanburg County. But this truck don't set right. She's loaded up heavy, she ought to ride good, but she don't. You know, after you've drove a semi, a beauty like the one I tore up, none of these regular jobs set right."

Ferd bounced gently in the seat, worked his hands and arms against the wheel, moved his head and chest back and fourth. He treated the truck as though it were an animal, able to receive and respond to infusions from his own centres; approached it with extra-mechanical energy, drawn from the deepest resources, the resources from which men control cards and dice. He was 'riding' it.

Crouching over the wheel, he shook his head in exasperation.

"She don't set right . . ."

One month the Spaniards rested and recovered then drew away northwestward winter came with snow and cold in Chicaca the Indians filtered through the guard attacked at night fired the huts where the Spaniards slept men unclothed and beasts unharnessed ran and trampled in confusion the Spaniards could not find arms and saddles De Soto alone mounted his horse killed an Indian then twisted and fell the girth had not been fastened had the attack been pressed the Spaniards would have been annihilated but it was dark the Indians were confused they thought the wild chaotic horses were cavalry in attack they fled. The town was in cinders many were without clothes polar winds swept unhindered down the centre of a continent the men tried to sleep by fires but one side burned while the other froze. Spring came a forge was set up harness saddles and weapons were made and repaired the Indians attacked again and the Spaniards placed foot soldiers in the front to spare the precious cavalry the Indians were driven off and the party pushed westward . .

Will turned again to the window, gazed passively at the truck farms. The land was mostly level, with some rolling hills, and it was good land. Even the small negro mule-farms with tumbling unpainted shacks seemed to produce well. Few trees survived, save in the towns where the highway might become, for a few moments, an avenue shaded with water oaks and Spanish moss. Beyond Will's view, to the northward, were the old Chickasaw country, and Yoknapatawpha County.

The truck passed over a river and Will lifted himself, gazed over the edge of the bridge at the turgid, slow-moving waters, reflecting the lowering clouds overhead . . .

The United States Government provided flatboats the John Cox the

Sliger Blue Buck Rainbow Squeezer and Moll Thompson on the Hiwassee River for those Indians who could be cajoled bribed corrupted into leaving their homes in the Old Smokies and going West four hundred and fifty came out of their cabins lived in barracks by the river while they waited bought dainties whiskey and trinkets sold their western land claims to speculators before departure the measles broke out the flatboats floated down the Hiwassee a young Lieutenant from West Point in command down the Tennessee through the Suck the Boiling-Pot the Skillet the Frying Pan measles raged through young and old but mostly young the government provided salt pork and white bread and no medicine at every stop the Indians went ashore to cut wood for coffins the whiskey vendors came on board at Waterloo Alabama the delay was long while the soldiers ploughed the Waterloo whores under way again one of the keelboats went down sixty-seven Cherokee rescued their belongings lost down the Tennessee the Ohio the Mississippi to the Whiskey Capitol of the emigration Fort Smith up the Arkansas but the water was low food put ashore but the boats would not float Indians put ashore but no wagons could be found the measles abated but it was hot country in the hot season fever season in the poisonous filth of the boat and shore camps cholera broke out the Indians scattered to the woods made their fires miles apart in terror of one another the doctor taken on in Alabama was dead in a week the young Lieutenant with what he had learned at West Point was alone to hunt doctors food wagons to feed and cure four hundred Indians a doctor came left in horror food was scarce the farmers would not sell their wagons it was planting time no one would approach no one but horse thieves the Lieutenant's horse was stolen he made his rounds over miles of woods on foot became ill stayed on his feet threw off the fever whites and half-breeds who had lost beloveds were weeping and wailing the Indians were silent digging graves wagons and teams were found for food and belongings infants and dying the rest marched on foot bloody and blistering to Indian Territory . . .

"Candy?"

The truck went over a bump as it passed off the bridge onto the land, and nausea stirred in the enormous emptiness of Will's stomach. He turned to see Ferd offering him a chocolate bar, already opened.

"Thanks," he said, his voice breaking. His hands trembled as he took the bar, broke it in two, and returned half.

Ferd held his piece a moment and gazed at Will, his eyes blue and bright and hard.

"You don't look like you've et in a month," he said.

Will laughed gently and held his eyes down. He was almost in tears. Ferd watched him a moment longer, and then turned to the road and chewed his candy. The truck droned on at a steady fifty.

The first sensation of chocolate and almond passed over Will's tongue was one of ineffable sweetness, a sweetness so long desired, so long unadmitted, as to be almost unbearable. He sucked on a corner of the bar like a baby, broke off only little pieces at a time, not so much to savor the taste but out of fear, fear the sweetness and the enjoyment of it would overwhelm him. Only slowly did he dare open himself to it.

"Thanks," he said again, his eyes damp and warm, gazing at the road.

Biting a larger piece, he sat back and closed his eyes, let the chocolate rest on his tongue, and melt. For some time he was still. Once he looked up, but the sun had broken through for a moment, and the bright reflection from the highway hurt his eyes. He closed them again. The drone of the motor, the gentle shaking of the truck, the consummate sweetness carried him, like an unwilled body floating in the waves, into sleep . . .

De Soto and the Spaniards came to a great river the largest they had seen they named it Rio Grande and some suggested it might even be larger than the Danube camp was set up and the men cut timber to make pirogues for a crossing Indians appeared in canopied barges and canoes parting the waters of the Great River like an armada of galleys the warriors painted and feathered in ochre and vermilion discharged arrows and retreated thirty days the Spaniards labored the pirogues were towed upstream that the landing would be opposite camp the crossing was made men and horses ferried across the Great River the pirogues were destroyed but the nails saved for future use. Westward the Christians faced captured a town took skins of the deer buffalo bear and wildcat made clothing for themselves and armour for the horses still westward harried by rebellious Indians bed clothing made from buffalo skins and winter came on the barren western plains with no maize slowly the numbers of men and horses diminished De Soto turned back toward the Great River for winter quarters but could not reach it passed the cold months in Autiamque learned from the Indians to trap rabbits. The interpreter died the Christians could not make themselves understood got wrong directions retraced their steps and wandered as spring came the rivers flooded men walked in swamps or swam dragging the horses finally reached the Great River scouts departed to search for the ocean but they could not pass the swamps the bogs the canebrakes and scrubs they returned and still men and horses diminished in numbers. De Soto sent word to the Cacique saying that he was the Child of the Sun and all men came to him to pay him tribute and in token of love and obedience the Cacique must come and bring him food and the Cacique replied as to what you say of your being the son of the Sun if you will cause him to dry up the Great River I will believe you as to the rest it is not my custom to visit anyone but rather all of whom I have ever heard have come to visit me to serve and obey me and pay me tribute whether voluntarily or by force if you desire to see me come where I am if for peace I will receive you with special goodwill if for war I will await you in my town but neither for you nor for any man will I set back one foot whereupon De Soto became despondent ill with fever kept the cavalry mounted day and night returned to a smaller town surprised killed and routed the Indians and with this lift to his waning reputation he sickened named Luis Moscoso Captain-General and died . . .

Will stirred, opened his eye. He was aware of deep sweetness and relaxation penetrating his body and limbs; of rest and relaxation barely initiated, richly and dreamily anticipated. Even the ache in his shoulder was encircled with a delicious tingling. The sun had gone in and the clouds were darker, more threatening than before. He didn't move, afraid to break the trance. Closing his eyes, he let the sound and motion of the truck restore him to sleep . . .

De Soto was buried at night the death hidden from the Indians who has been told he was immortal but the Indians missed him discovered the grave the body was taken up carried at night in a canoe and dropped in the Great River still the Indians asked for him Moscoso said he had ascended into the heavens as he had many times before and would return the Cacique sent two Indians to be beheaded that they might join the Governor in the heavens and serve him and Moscoso cursed their heathen practices. De Soto's property was distributed on credit to be payed for out of gold and silver yet to be discovered and again the Spaniards turned westward many were glad De Soto was dead he had driven them onward into Florida but they were anxious to reach New Spain by way of land and get out of Florida they had had enough all but one who stayed behind with his Indian concubine for fear of losing her in payment of gambling debts still the Indians attacked and men and horses slowly diminished in numbers. As before the towns became thin the maize scarce winter was coming westward lay only desert and wild homeless Indians who lived as the Spaniards said like Arabs again the Christians turned headed for the Great River where the soil nourished by abundant waters produced quantities of maize they would build brigantines and in the spring would sail down the river and out of the continent of Florida forever Moscoso wanted only to reach a place where for once he could get his full measure of sleep. Back to the river they struggled through towns they had already devastated what little food remained the Indians had hidden reaching the river they found no maize the Indians in fear of them had not planted in driving cold and rain through flooded waters and north wind carrying their sick they came to Aminoya where old stores of maize were found and the harried Christians camped for the winter . . .

    Will opened his eyes and was still for a moment, uncomprehending. The world seemed to have closed upon him. The cab was hot and tight, filled with smoke; both windows were shut. The drone of the motor was buried in the sound of thunder and of a torrential rain that tumbled out of the clouds, rain falling not in drops but in globes, graying the air, clattering against glass and steel. The windshield wiper arched back and forth, useless and persistent.

Ferd was crouching over the wheel, smoking, driving much slower. From time to time he rubbed the windshield with his sleeve. Seeing Will awake he turned to him, moving only his head, and smiled, the hard lines of his mouth drawing back, the cigarette trembling in the corner.

"I guess you ain't slept in a month, neither," he said.

Will laughed a little and sat up.

"I feel better."

Kicking among the junk on the floor he found a rag moderately clean and picked it up, wiped the full width of the windshield. Ferd nodded his thanks.

"This'll quit arter a while. It's a river rain. Delta rain. Comes down in tubs and then quits and the sun comes out and it'll be hotter than ever."

Will opened his window a crack for air. A litle rain came in and felt good on his face.

"Man, I hate this weather," Ferd continued. "Don't see how they stand it. My home's the mountains. I guess once you lived up there you can't never get used to this low country. Know what I do first thing when I get back up yonder? Stop by a stream some place and get a drink of water. Cool, fresh mountain water! Nothing like it!"

The rain let up a little and the wiper began to make headway with the floods on the windshield. Thunder threatened remotely, withdrawing. Will ate some more of his candy bar.

"How long was I out?" he asked.

"Not long. Half hour, maybe. But you slept good."

Ferd was concentrating on the road, stepping up his speed.

Through the window Will made out changes in the countryside.

The level farmland was gone, had given way to short broken hills, bluff hills, many of them wooded. The highway rolled and turned and passed through deep cuts. We must be near the river, Will thought.

The rain exhausted itself abruptly, and almost at once the sun came out. It was not a pure sun but filtered through clouds, glaring. Steam rose from the truck and highway, and isolated showers, tiny spray drops glistening in the sunlight, drifted and fell erratically. Will and Ferd opened their windows, let the hot wet air drive the smoke from the cab. Ferd sat up straight and resumed his orginal speed, where the road permitted.

They drove in silence for a short while. Will was aware that Ferd was glancing calculatingly at the snapshots over the windshield. He couldn't seem to make up his mind. Suddenly his arm shot out and he pointed to the one at the end, directly in front of Will.

"See that one?"

Will looked at head, shoulders and well-developed figure of a young girl. She had a posed smile, and a self-willed face.

"Take her down and look at her."

Will took the snapshot from its place and held it before him.

"How old would you say she was?"

"About eighteen," Will guessed.

"Thirteen when that was took. She's fifteen now. Been getting the curse since she was ten."

He paused, glancing back and forth between picture and road. Then he turned wholly to the road, gripping the wheel.

"Jailbait," he barked, between tight-drawn lips.

Will continued to look at the picture.

"You know, there ain't nothing about that gal but what you see right there." He spoke tensely. "What I mean, just to look at and put into bed. That's all. She's the orneriest brat this side of the river. Lives alone with her aunt, down the road from us. The old woman works all day to support her and then comes home and cooks dinner, cleans the house, does the washing, the ironing and the dishes and then like as not sets down and makes a dress for her. That one just sets around after school and suns herself. Week-ends she'll go to the drive-in or the square dance, flirt with the married men, fool around with other gal's fellows. Their house ain't half finished but she's got to have a hunk of her aunt's dough to go to town every week, take dancing lessons, buy candy and new clothes and go to the movies. Sometimes I guess the old woman figures it an investment. But she's going to get a shock some day: if the kid ever does strike it rich her aunt will be somebody she ain't never heard of. And you know there ain't nothing you can tell her. She tells my wife jokes and the wife comes home and tells me and you'd think she just come out of the stable. What I mean, she knows it all. If my little woman knew I even had that picture up here she'd cut my throat."

He turned to the window and spat out the cigarett butt.

"Man, there ain't nothing to recommend her. Nothing but what she's got under that sweater."

He was silent for a while, watching the road. His eyes for the first time lost their brightness. Unconsciously he slowed the truck, and the motor became quieter.

"But you know, it's a funny thing," he went on. "I know all that. Knew it the first time I met the kid. It don't take long to find out what folks are up to, just the way they act is enough. She's a bitch. There ain't nothing she's ever done or most likely ever will do that'll make me change her out of the damnedest bitch in forty-eight states. But you know what? That kid's got me. Silly, ain't it? It's the truth. Deep down plum inside me, I've been took. There ain't a thing nasty enough you can say about her in front of me: but if she'd have me I'd crawl into the hay with her tomorrow. I'd do just about anything she wanted to name so's I could have her just once. I'd sleep with her right in her own home or just whatever place she wanted to pick out. I'd work sixteen hours a day seven days a week just to spend a half hour at night with her, and her out flirting around the rest of the time. I'd go plum to hell and sit there twenty years if I thought she'd be in my bed when I got back."

He sat soberly at the wheel, still driving slowly. The sun suddenly vanished and the clouds threatened again. The hills became dark and the luminosity vanished from the highway. Fresh thunder rumbled ahead of them.

"Do you know what she thinks of me?" Ferd asked, speaking with more confidence. "Nothing. Plain dirt nothing. I could drop this truck into the Mississippi River and she wouldn't care if I never come up. Let me tell you something else. The first time I got to know this kid she set her sights for me. Didn't give a damn about me and still don't, just wanted to break me down, get me on her list. She started flirting right out in broad daylight. Just a kid you know. The wife and I used to laugh about it, she was so damn flat-footed. Then something happened. All of a sudden something sprung in me. All this flirting and swishing her hips and coming over to say hello in a bathing suit and worrying her plunging neckline all over the kitchen began to take. I couldn't tell you what happened or even when it happened. It's like she was building up this charge against me, just a little bit every day, piling it up and piling it up. At first it didn't look like much and I laughed at it; then I quit paying heed because it went on just the same all the time. Until one day I turned around and I just couldn't stand it no more, the charge had got too big, and the lightning struck. Only it wasn't like that because it just happened, I didn't know nothing about it. From then on, didn't matter what we was before, leastways as far as I was concerned, we were stuck."

Lightning flashed across the highway and the rain burst upon them, pouring in great floods as before. Thunder roared overhead. They rolled up the windows quickly, and Will replaced the photograph over the windshield. Ferd glanced at it as he saw it restored.

"Now she's got me on the hook she just gives me the light

treatment." He was leaning toward Will, talking louder, almost shouting to drown out the rain. "Keep me irritated, keep me coming. Maybe she's been to town and bought herself a new playsuit. She's got to come over and show us how the halter snaps in back and the elastic in it is too tight and makes a line in front and how the skirt swirls up when she turns around and the tights are nothing but a little old netting and you can see her white panties underneath riding up to her hips. Once or twice she's let me get close to her. Put my arm on her shoulder, or sneak a kiss."

Will began to withdraw slowly to the far side of the seat. There was a strange sensation in the cab. The windows were shut up tight, the air was hot and close, the windshield began to fog again. The drone of the motor, the pelting of the rain, the rumbling of thunder intensified the sense of enclosure, of being in a compartment, insufferably tight, projected through nameless atmosphere. The sound of Ferd's voice became almost unbearable. The words, the vowels seemed to form into physical objects as they left his mouth, roaring and echoing back and forth in the cab, striking the steel and glass in response to the raindrops on the outside. Will felt as though his head were swelling, as though it nearly filled the space of the cab, and the heat of the motor, the reverberations, the suddenly intolerable presence of Ferd existed in a space encompassed by his own physical being.

"Once we was playing cards, me and her and the wife. I put my hand on her knee, under the table, and started to move up. She caught it between her legs and squeezed them together, held it there. That's as close as I ever got. Or ever will get, I reckon. She don't have to let me get no closer. Just keep me swinging, like a fish she's got all hooked up and she's just too damn lazy to pull into the boat."

Will opened the window a crack. His chest was heaving, he was breathing hard. The hills were thickly wooded with a variety of trees. Suddenly the space opened and they come to a network of interlocking roads: the entrance to Vicksburg National Military

The river flows through soft alluvial mud intersected for twenty miles on either side by a web a maze of interlocking and obstructed bayous

the banks overgrown with a wild jungle tangle the intervening spaces sunken in swamps it is the crookedest big river in the world also the orneriest changing or refusing to change its course at will this was the problem that faced Grant the river that must be opened to New Orleans to cut off Confederate supplies isolate the Rebels from their granary in the West open now to St. Louis to Cairo to Memphis but at Vicksburg the bluff hills rise two hundred feet the highest and strongest point on the river terraced and fortified with entrenched batteries so that no ships could pass. Vicksburg the Hill City protected south and west by the river north by the fortifications at Hayne's Bluff could only be attacked in the rear in the tail that is from the east Grant approached from the north moving slowly to keep open his supplies food forage and ammunition via railroad and river but the rail lines were broken by raids stores destroyed and Grant retreated he approached from the west tried to dig a canal in the peninsula opposite Vicksburg so the fleet could by-pass the batteries but the river refused to stay out of the work finally flooded the operation the soldiers had to withdraw or be drowned Grant tried to open a passage through the bayous but the Rebels felled trees across them in all his efforts he had failed with his northern soldiers suffering the terrors not only of the terrain but of the climate the pestilential fevers the drinking water on which the Confederates thrived. Grant crossed the river above Vicksburg to the western shore made corduroy roads moved southward through swamps bogs canebrakes over bayous to the river below Vicksburg some of the fleet protected by gunboats moving at night without lights ran the batteries at Vicksburg the Confederates fired houses to illuminate the river but the ships passed brought supplies to Grant below the city and ferried his army across the river back to the eastern shore forty three thousand men ready to strike. The supply line past Vicksburg was difficult he must move fast subdue Jackson and Vicksburg re-open securer lines from the north when Washington heard of his plans they were promptly countermanded but Grant had left before the order arrived holding his army together with none to protect the rear he broke from his only source of supplies the river the men carried five days rations foraging parties went out at night to scavenge on the land find corn and poultry on the plantations feinting north at Vicksburg the army moved northeast to Jackson a manoever without precedent in modern warfare an army moving as a unit cut off by its own volition from supplies and sources a man projected willfully into alien country to which he has not been invited subject constantly to destruction depending on mobility subsisting on the food scavenged from day to day off the difficult resistent land. Grant routed the Confederate army at Jackson left the city devastated the railroads destroyed for twenty miles in all directions turned and headed west over the main route toward the bluff hills to strike Vicksburg the fortress on the river from the east routed the Rebels at Champion's Hill captured the batteries at Hayne's Bluff above the city opened supply lines to the north via the river and the men rejoicing to quit the plantation diet of chicken turkey and cornbread return to hardtack and bacon attacked the fortified eastern lines of Vicksburg . . .

The rain slackened, and stopped abruptly, as before. The sun remained hidden but spread a dull glare over the land. Will opened his window, breathed deeply, more easily.

Ferd was silent, morose, opening his window absently. He drove with mechanical caution as the highway passed through the Park, under the Memorial Arch and into the city of Vicksburg.

. . . but the Rebels had dug in repulsed the Federals in two days of bloody attacks three thousand dead and wounded lay between the close lines the Federals dug in for a siege neither side would yield to bury the dead the fighting went on it was late May under a burning sun the corpses stank the stench climbing the fortified hills to the noses of the Rebels fearing an epidemic they called an armistice and the dead were buried while officers of two sides conversed and joked exchanging views regarding the siege trading news for smokes. The work done the men returned to their entrenchments the siege began the Federals supplied by the river to the north poured shrapnel mortar and Parrott shells grape shot canister grenades and musketry into the city the residents dug caves in the hillsides cavediggers were in demand brought good wages the ladies would go to Sky Parlor Hill or stand on their verandas to watch the fireworks when the shattering iron came too close they retired to their caves learned to cook eat sleep in them troglodytes lying sitting or crouching in darkness listening to the rattle of musketry the distant whistling of a

71

shell coming closer screaming rushing waiting for the explosion wondering then the electric shock the sickening jolting the shaking cave supports the sifting dirt people who have crawled back into caves into the earth longing for the thrill and priviledge of once more standing erect. Unfed dogs wandered in the streets and the Rebels stayed in the trenches day and night sun and rain unable to stand or sleep their rations brought to them the stocks were low half rations quarter rations then a biscuit a day hunger and then scurvy a cow a horse an ox wandering to the hills for grass killed by wandering shrapnel went into the hands of speculators rats were eaten the soldiers rojoiced when fresh-dead mule came on the rations the wounded caught between the lines were left to rot and die moaning rolling slowly back and forth begging for a drink of fresh water the Federals worked at night digging closer trenches mining exploding Confederate lines so close were the lines that insults jokes and wisecracks brother to brother shared the air with shrapnel more guns and men came down the river to Grant an armistice was called the silence in the caves the trenches the shelled streets and homes was awful. Starved and overpowered the city surrendered on the fourth day of July opened itself to the east while the soldiers wept the invaders entered and in the words of Abraham Lincoln the Father of Waters rolled unvexed to the sea . . .

    Near the centre of Vicksburg Ferd took a left turn, following the highway markers, and it was not long before Will had his first view of the river. They were driving southward, parallel to it, and the great bridge that they would cross from Mississippi to Louisiana loomed ahead, built high over the river, but mightier in its length over the broadness of the river, than in its height. The sun broke through again and the clouds began to dispel: the city became blanketed with heat. Will watched the low, even flow of the river, as Ferd drove on in silence . . .

The forge was set up the iron collars the slave chains were gathered also the iron in ammunition all were melted down beaten into nails timber was felled a Portuguese who had learned to saw lumber as a slave in Fez taught the art to four Biscayan carpenters who hewed the planks and ribs a Genoese and Sardinian caulked with oakum from henequen also with flax with ravellings from the

Indian shawls the cooper became sick almost died but recovered labored while still sick made two half-hogsheads for water the Indians brought fish for food also shawls for sails and watched the work. The river began to rise the town was encircled the cavalry became useless the Indians out-numbered the Christians but still they brought fish and shawls and ropes cables were made from mulberry bark anchors from stirrups the river rose covered the ground in March and the work stopped rafts were made strewn with boughs for the horses the men lived in the lofts of their huts traveled in canoes and still the Indians came to look at the ships. Moscoso had an Indian captured tortured he revealed a plot of attack when thirty Indians came with fish Moscoso cut off their right hands sent them back others came their right hands and noses were cut off Moscoso boasted to the Caciques that they could not have so much as a warlike thought that he did not know about in advance the plot was broken but the Indians were starving for want of the maize the Spaniards had taken they came begging thin and weak Moscoso forbade feeding them but they were so pitiful many of the men gave them maize on the sly in return for work on the ships. In June the brigantines and pirogues were finished it pleased God for the river to rise again and the ships were floated into deep water twenty-two of the finest horses were put on board the rest killed the meat jerked along with that of the hogs and put on board early in July four years after the first landing in Puerto del Espiritu Santo the Christians their numbers reduced by half their ships without slaves or gold pushed into the tide of the Great River the waters flooding through the continent of Florida washing the body of the Adelantado De Soto and headed for the open waters beyond . . .

Will kept his eyes on the oceanic expanse of the river and on the great bridge looming ahead. It became easy to imagine that the truck was stationary, rolling on a treadmill, while the bridge moved, turning, changing perspective, jockeying and disciplining its length into position to pass under the wheels of the truck. The very size of the bridge lent itself to this illusion.

"Reckon I'll give 'em up," Ferd said abruptly. "All of 'em. Quit fooling around. If that kid comes over and starts throwing herself in my face I'll just go out back, start fooling with the truck. Give her the cold shoulder."

He took out his cigarettes and lit one for himself, absently. As he was about to put them away he remembered Will, and offered them.

"Thanks," said Will, accepting.

"After all, I got the cutest little wife in the world. I got a fine kid and another one on the way. I'll just quit fooling with all these others and stick to home. Stay out of trouble."

He raised himself, crouched a moment over the wheel, and sat back in a more confidant posture.

"Fellow's only got one life. If you wreck that they ain't going to hand out another. Reckon I'll play it straight. I'm going to get that house paid off, then I'm going to trade in this hunk of junk, buy me another semi like the one I tore up. She'll be as good or better."

He nodded authoritatively to himself.

"Arter all, a fellow can't hope to get out of debt when he's got his mind on other things. . ."

Indians escorted them in canoes a short distance then retreated the Christians put ashore for the night set out in the morning they came to an empty town helped themselves to maize and stopped to shell it Indians attacked and were driven off. The Christians set out again were followed through the day by Indians in canoes stopped for the night in an open field and the Indians fled but the next day they were followed by more than a hundred Indian canoes spread in formation across the breadth of the Great River a curtain on the flood waters rushing the Christians from the continent some of the canoes detached themselves paddled downstream to attack and the pirogues moved upstream to meet them but the brigantines could not follow in hand-to-hand fighting the pirogues capsized the Spaniards in their iron armour sank to the bottom. The ships stayed on the river through the night next day the fleet of canoes still followed they attacked the brigantines one at a time from one ship to another the Spaniards without armour were easy targets dropped their oars scurried to the bottom boards the ship began to swing crazily until the steersman guarded by one armoured shielded Christian took his oar the Spaniards found their sleeping mats withstood the arrows they hung them around the brigantines returned to their oars but the Indians lofted their arrows arched them into the sky and they fell over the mats and into the ships. Through the day the night and into the next day the attacks continued the war crys screaming across the waters so the Spaniards could not rest when a ship lagged the Indians clustered upon it until the oarsmen strained themselves and regained the others at a border of territories the warriors retreated and warriors of the new territory took up the chase thus the chain of attack was unbroken as in the earlier days the chain of slaves had been unbroken. The horses slowed the ships their pirogues were easy prey the Spaniards stopped to slaughter them the last of the Spanish cavalry the great beast that had carried the Christians over body of land and Indian the meat was jerked and taken aboard and at last after days of harrying warfare the Indians retreated and were not replaced by others the men rested on their oars floated peacefully under the summer sun down the broadening river. At the very mouth with the open welcoming waters spreading before them they put onto the sandy shore and once more Indians appeared rushed in to attack and withdraw beyond range of the crossbow the Spaniards helpless without horses retired to their ships and left the shore left the brown waters muddy with the land that had driven them out the land that had given them nothing but hardship hunger and warfare had destroyed their equipment their clothes the ornaments of their belief and left them to live like the Indians who inhabited it the land that save for a mighty arterial flooding stream might have swallowed and destroyed them. They quit the brown waters without regret and entered the blue . . .

The truck started across the bridge. Will looked to the north, toward the city, the junction of the Yazoo Canal and the river at the point of De Soto Island.

This is the first of my borders, he thought. The river that splits a nation. I have left the East behind. The rock cave in the Smokies where I spent the first night has projected me this far across the land: I have wandered and scavenged and begged my way to the Mississippi, and I have not turned. This river is the first of my borders. Now there is more land and another border, another river, dividing land and people, a river that bears the name once given to these waters: the Rio Grande . . .

Following the coast the Spaniards set out for New Spain some were blown out to sea ran out of water but they made land and beached the ships a south wind came up the brigantines were almost wrecked but water was taken on and the voyage begun again high winds were followed by a calm mosquitos appeared the sails were black with them the men's faces and bodies swollen in welts the ships parted and came together fair weather returned and the Christians put ashore to hold service on the beach by way of thanks. Sailing under fair skies they came at last to the Rio de Panico where they put ashore discovered Christian Indians who told them of a Christian town the men rejoiced went wild on the beach fell to their knees kissed the sand they were like children rabid with joy after four and one half bitter years without conquest or gold crowding to a land where the Cross the Holy Spirit the Virgin were worshipped a land of their own kind . . .